CHILDREN

OF THE

NEW WORLD

CHILDREN

OF THE

NEW WORLD

| *Stories* |

Alexander Weinstein

PICADOR

New York

CHILDREN OF THE NEW WORLD. Copyright © 2016 by Alexander Weinstein. All rights reserved. Printed in the United States of America. For information, address Picador, 175 Fifth Avenue, New York, N.Y. 10010.

picadorusa.com • picadorbookroom.tumblr.com
twitter.com/picadorusa • facebook.com/picadorusa

Picador® is a U.S. registered trademark and is used by Macmillan Publishing Group, LLC, under license from Pan Books Limited.

For book club information, please visit facebook.com/picadorbookclub or e-mail marketing@picadorusa.com.

The following stories have been previously published, and a number have appeared in different form: "Saying Goodbye to Yang," in *Zahir;* "The Cartographers," in *Chattahoochee Review;* "Heartland," in *Pleiades;* "Excerpts from *The New World Authorized Dictionary*," in *Cream City Review;* "Children of the New World," in *Pleiades;* "A Brief History of the Failed Revolution," in *Infinity's Kitchen;* "Migration," in *PRISM International;* "The Pyramid and the Ass," in *A Cappella Zoo;* "Rocket Night," in *Southern Indiana Review;* "Openness," in *Beloit Fiction Journal;* "Ice Age," in *Natural Bridge.*

Library of Congress Cataloging-in-Publication Data

Names: Weinstein, Alexander author.
Title: Children of the new world : stories / Alexander Weinstein.
Description: First edition. | New York : Picador, 2016.
Identifiers: LCCN 2016019224 (print) | LCCN 2016027252 (ebook) |
    ISBN 9781250098993 (trade pbk.) | ISBN 9781250099006 (e-book)
Classification: LCC PS3623.E4324467 A6 2016 (print) |
    LCC PS3623.E4324467 (ebook) | DDC 813/.6—dc23
LC record available at https://lccn.loc.gov/2016019224

Our books may be purchased in bulk for promotional, educational, or business use. Please contact your local bookseller or the Macmillan Corporate and Premium Sales Department at 1-800-221-7945, extension 5442, or by e-mail at MacmillanSpecial Markets@macmillan.com.

First Edition: September 2016

10 9 8 7 6 5 4 3 2 1

For Peter

CONTENTS

CHILDREN

OF THE

NEW WORLD

SAYING GOODBYE TO YANG

WE'RE SITTING AROUND the table eating Cheerios—my wife sipping tea, Mika playing with her spoon, me suggesting apple picking over the weekend—when Yang slams his head into his cereal bowl. It's a sudden mechanical movement, and it splashes cereal and milk all over the table. Yang rises, looking as though nothing odd just occurred, and then he slams his face into the bowl again. Mika thinks this is hysterical. She starts mimicking Yang, bending over to dunk her own face in the milk, but Kyra's pulling her away from the table and whisking her out of the kitchen so I can take care of Yang.

At times like these, I'm not the most clearheaded. I stand in my kitchen, my chair knocked over behind me, at a total loss. Shut him down, call the company? Shut him down, call the company? By now the bowl is empty, milk dripping off the table, Cheerios all over the goddamned place, and Yang has a red ring on his forehead from where his face has been striking the bowl. A bit of skin has pulled away from his skull over his left eyelid. I decide I need to shut him down; the company can walk me through the reboot. I get behind Yang and untuck his shirt from his pants as he jerks forward, then I push the release button on his back panel. The thing's screwed shut and won't pop open.

"Kyra," I say loudly, turning toward the doorway to the living room. No answer, just the sound of Mika upstairs, crying to see her brother, and the concussive thuds of Yang hitting his head against the table. "Kyra!"

"What is it?" she yells back. *Thud.*

"I need a Phillips head!"

"What?" *Thud.*

"A screwdriver!"

"I can't get it! Mika's having a tantrum!" *Thud.*

"Great, thanks!"

Kyra and I aren't usually like this. We're a good couple, communicative and caring, but moments of crisis bring out the worst in us. The skin above Yang's left eye has completely split, revealing the white membrane beneath. There's no time for me to run to the basement for my toolbox. I grab a butter knife from the table and attempt to use the tip as a screwdriver. The edge, however, is too wide, completely useless against the small metal cross of the screw, so I jam the knife into the back panel and pull hard. There's a cracking noise, and a piece of flesh-colored Bioplastic skids across the linoleum as I flip open Yang's panel. I push the power button and wait for the dim blue light to shut off. With alarming still-ness, Yang sits upright in his chair, as though something is amiss, and cocks his head toward the window. Outside, a car-dinal takes off from the branch where it was sitting. Then, with an internal sigh, Yang slumps forward, chin dropping to his chest. The illumination beneath his skin extinguishes, giving his features a sickly ashen hue.

I hear Kyra coming down the stairs with Mika. "Is Yang okay?"

"Don't come in here!"

"Mika wants to see her brother."

"Stay out of the kitchen! Yang's not doing well!" The kitchen wall echoes with the muffled footsteps of my wife and daughter returning upstairs.

"Fuck," I say under my breath. Not doing well? Yang's a piece of crap and I just destroyed his back panel. God knows how much those cost. I get out my cell and call Brothers & Sisters Inc. for help.

※

WHEN WE ADOPTED Mika three years ago, it seemed like the progressive thing to do. We considered it our one small strike against cloning. Kyra and I are both white, middle-class, and have lived an easy and privileged life; we figured it was time to give something back to the world. It was Kyra who sug-gested she be Chinese. The earthquake had left thousands of orphans in its wake, Mika among them. It was hard not to agree. My main concern—one I voiced to Kyra privately, and quite vocally to the adoption agency during our interview— was the cultural differences. The most I knew about China came from the photos and "Learn Chinese" translations on the place mats at Golden Dragon. The adoption agency suggested purchasing Yang.

"He's a Big Brother, babysitter, and storehouse of cultural knowledge all in one," the woman explained. She handed us a colorful pamphlet—*China!* it announced in red dragon-shaped letters—and said we should consider. We considered. Kyra was putting in forty hours a week at Crate & Barrel, and I was still managing double shifts at Whole Foods. It was true, we were going to need someone to take care of Mika, and there was no way we were going to use some clone from the neighborhood. Kyra and I weren't egocentric enough to consider ourselves worth replicating, nor did we want our neighbors' *perfect* kids making our daughter feel insecure. In addition, Yang came with a breadth of cultural knowledge that Kyra and I could never match. He was programmed with grades K through college, and had an in-depth understanding of national Chinese holidays like flag-raising ceremonies and Ghost Festivals. He knew about moon cakes and sky lanterns. For two hundred more, we could upgrade to a model that would teach Mika tai chi and acupressure when she got older. I thought about it. "I could learn Mandarin," I said as we lay in bed that night. "Come on," Kyra said, "there's no fucking way that's happening." So I squeezed her hand and said, "Okay, it'll be two kids then."

※

HE CAME TO us fully programmed; there wasn't a baseball game, pizza slice, bicycle ride, or movie that I could introduce him to. Early on I attempted such outings to create a sense of companionship, as though Yang were a foreign exchange student in our home. I took him to see the Tigers play in Comerica Park. He sat and ate peanuts with me, and when he saw me cheer, he followed suit and put his hands in the air, but there was no sense that he was enjoying the experience. Ultimately, these attempts at camaraderie, from visiting haunted houses to tossing a football around the backyard, felt awkward—as though Yang were humoring me—and so, after a couple months, I gave up. He lived with us, ate food, privately dumped his stomach canister, brushed his teeth, read Mika goodnight stories, and went to sleep when we shut off the lights.

All the same, he was an important addition to our lives. You could always count on him to keep conversation going with some fact about China that none of us knew. I remember driving with him, listening to *World Drum* on NPR, when he said from the backseat, "This song utilizes the xun, an ancient Chinese instrument organized around minor third intervals." Other times, he'd tell us Fun Facts. Like one afternoon, when we'd all gotten ice cream at Old World Creamery, he turned to Mika and said, "Did you know ice cream was invented in China over four thousand years ago?" His delivery of this info was a bit mechanical—a linguistic trait we attempted to keep Mika from adopting. There was a lack of passion to his statements, as though he wasn't interested in the facts. But Kyra and I understood this to be the result of his being an early model, and when one considered the moments when he'd turn to Mika and say, "I love you, little sister," there was no way to deny what an integral part of our family he was.

❋

TWENTY MINUTES OF hold-time later, I'm informed that Brothers & Sisters Inc. isn't going to replace Yang. My warranty ran out eight months ago, which means I've got a broken Yang, and if I want telephone technical support, it's going to cost me thirty dollars a minute now that I'm post-warranty. I hang up. Yang is still slumped with his chin on his chest. I go over and push the power button on his back, hoping all he needed was to be restarted. Nothing. There's no blue light, no sound of his body warming up.

Shit, I think. There goes eight thousand dollars.

"Can we come down yet?" Kyra yells.

"Hold on a minute!" I pull Yang's chair out and place my arms around his waist. It's the first time I've actually embraced Yang, and the coldness of his skin surprises me.

While he has lived with us almost as long as Mika, I don't think anyone besides her has ever hugged or kissed him. There have been times when, as a joke, one of us might nudge Yang with an elbow and say something humorous like, "Lighten up, Yang!" but that's been the extent of our contact. I hold him close to me now, bracing my feet solidly beneath my body, and lift. He's heavier than I imagined, his weight that of the eighteen-year-old boy he's designed to be. I hoist him onto my shoulder and carry him through the living room out to the car.

My neighbor, George, is next door raking leaves. George is a friendly enough guy, but completely unlike us. Both his children are clones, and he drives a hybrid with a bumper sticker that reads IF I WANTED TO GO SOLAR, I'D GET A TAN. He looks up as I pop the trunk. "That Yang?" he asks, leaning against his rake.

"Yeah," I say and lower Yang into the trunk.

"No shit. What's wrong with him?"

"Don't know. One moment we're sitting having breakfast, the next he's going haywire. I had to shut him down, and he won't start up again."

"Jeez. You okay?"

"Yeah, I'm fine," I say instinctively, though as I answer, I realize that I'm not. My legs feel wobbly and the sky above us seems thinner, as though there's less air. Still, I'm glad I answered as I did. A man who paints his face for Super Bowl games isn't the type of guy to open your heart to.

"You got a technician?" George asks.

"Actually, no. I was going to take him over to Quick Fix and see—"

"Don't take him there. I've got a good technician, took Tiger there when he wouldn't fetch. The guy's in Kalamazoo, but it's worth the drive." George takes a card from his wallet. "He'll check Yang out and fix him for a third of what those guys at Q-Fix will charge you. Tell Russ I sent you."

✻

RUSS GOODMAN'S TECH Repair Shop is located two miles off the highway amid a row of industrial warehouses. The place is wedged between Mike's Muffler Repair and a storefront called Stacey's Second Times—a cluttered thrift store displaying old rifles, iPods, and steel bear traps in its front window. Two men in caps and oil-stained plaid shirts are standing in front smoking cigarettes. As I park alongside the rusted mufflers and oil drums of Mike's, they eye my solar car like they would a flea-ridden dog.

"Hi there, I'm looking for Russ Goodman," I say as I get out. "I called earlier."

The taller of the two, a middle-aged man with gray stubble and weathered skin, nods to the other guy to end their conversation. "That'd be me," he says. I'm ready to shake his hand, but he just takes a drag from his cigarette stub and says, "Let's see what you got," so I pop the trunk instead. Yang is lying alongside my jumper cables and windshield-washing fluid with his legs folded beneath him. His head is twisted at an unnatural angle, as though he were trying to turn his chin onto the other side of his shoulder. Russ stands next to me, with his thick forearms and a smell of tobacco, and lets out a sigh. "You brought a Korean." He says this as a statement of fact. Russ is the type of person I've made a point to avoid in my life: a guy that probably has a WE CLONE OUR OWN sticker on the back of his truck.

"He's Chinese," I say.

"Same thing," Russ says. He looks up and gives the other man a shake of his head. "Well," he says heavily, "bring him inside, I'll see what's wrong with him." He shakes his head again as he walks away and enters his shop.

Russ's shop consists of a main desk with a telephone and cash register, across from which stands a table with a coffee-maker, Styrofoam cups, and powdered creamer. Two vinyl chairs sit by a table with magazines on it. The door to the workroom is open. "Bring him back here," Russ says. Carrying Yang over my shoulder, I follow him into the back room.

The work space is full of body parts, switchboards, cables, and tools. Along the wall hang disjointed arms, a couple of knees, legs of different sizes, and the head of a young girl, about seventeen, with long red hair. There's a worktable cluttered with patches of skin and a Pyrex box full of female hands. All the skin tones are Caucasian. In the middle of the room is an old massage table streaked with grease. Probably something Russ got from Stacey's Seconds. "Go 'head and lay him down there," Russ says. I place Yang down on his stomach and position his head in the small circular face rest at the top of the table.

"I don't know what happened to him," I say. "He's always been fine, then this morning he started malfunctioning. He was slamming his head onto the table over and over." Russ doesn't say anything. "I'm wondering if it might be a problem with his hard drive," I say, feeling like an idiot. I've got no clue what's wrong with him; it's just something George mentioned I should check out. I should have gone to Quick Fix. The young techies with their polished manners always make me feel more at ease. Russ still hasn't spoken. He takes a mallet from the wall and a Phillips head screwdriver. "Do you think it's fixable?"

"We'll see. I don't work on imports," he says, meeting my eyes for the first time since I've arrived, "but, since you know George, I'll open him up and take a look. Go 'head and take a seat out there."

"How long do you think it'll take?"

"Won't know till I get him opened up," Russ says, wiping his hands on his jeans.

"Okay," I say meekly and leave Yang in Russ's hands.

In the waiting room I pour myself a cup of coffee and stir in some creamer. I set my cup on the coffee table and look through the magazines. There's *Guns & Ammo, Tech Repair, Brothers & Sisters Digest*—I put the magazines back down. The wall behind the desk is cluttered with photos of Russ and his kids, all of whom look exactly like him, and, buried among these, a small sign with an American flag on it and the message THERE AIN'T NO YELLOW IN THE RED, WHITE, AND BLUE.

"Pssh," I say instinctually, letting out an annoyed breath of air. This was the kind of crap that came out during the invasion of North Korea, back when the nation changed the color of its ribbons from yellow to blue. Ann Arbor's a progressive city, but even there, when Kyra and I would go out with Yang and Mika in public, there were many who avoided eye contact. Stop the War activists weren't any different. It was that first Christmas, as Kyra, Yang, Mika, and I were at the airport being individually searched, that I realized Chinese, Japanese, South Korean didn't matter anymore; they'd all become threats in the eyes of Americans. I decide not to sit here looking at Russ's racist propaganda, and leave to check out the bear traps at Stacey's.

※

"HE'S DEAD," RUSS tells me. "I can replace his insides, more or less build him back from scratch, but that's gonna cost you about as much as a used one."

I stand looking at Yang, who's lying on the massage table with a tangle of red and green wires protruding from his back. Even though his skin has lost its vibrant color, it still looks soft, like when he first came to our home. "Isn't there anything else you can do?"

"His voice box and language system are still running. If you want, I'll take it out for you. He'll be able to talk to her, there just won't be any face attached. Cost you sixty bucks." Russ is wiping his hands on a rag, avoiding my eyes. I think of the sign hanging in the other room. Sure, I think, I can just imagine the pleasure Russ will take in cutting up Yang.

"No, that's all right. I'll just take him home. What do I owe you?"

"Nothing," Russ says. I look up at him. "You know George," he says as explanation. "Besides, I can't fix him for you."

On the ride home, I call Kyra. She picks up on the second ring.

"Hello?"

"Hey, it's me." My voice is ragged.

"Are you okay?"

"Yeah," I say, then add, "Actually, no."

"What's the matter? How's Yang?"

"I don't know. The tech I took him to says he's dead, but I don't believe him—the guy had a thing against Asians. I'm thinking about taking Yang over to Quick Fix." There's silence on the other end of the line. "How's Mika?" I ask.

"She keeps asking if Yang's okay. I put a movie on for her. . . . Dead?" she asks. "Are you positive?"

"No, I'm not sure. I don't know. I'm not ready to give up

on him yet. Look," I say, glancing at the dash clock, "it's only three. I'm going to suck it up and take him to Quick Fix. I'm sure if I drop enough cash they can do something."

"What will we do if he's dead?" Kyra asks. "I've got work on Monday."

"We'll figure it out," I say. "Let's just wait until I get a second opinion."

Kyra tells me she loves me, and I return my love, and we hang up. It's as my Bluetooth goes dead that I feel the tears coming. I remember last fall when Kyra was watching Mika. I was in the garage taking down the rake when, from behind me, I heard Yang. He stood awkwardly in the doorway, as though he was uncertain what to do while Mika was being taken care of. "Can I help you?" he asked.

On that chilly late afternoon, with the red and orange leaves falling around us—me in my vest, and Yang in the black suit he came with—Yang and I quietly raked leaves into large piles on the flat earth until the backyard looked like a village of leaf huts. Then Yang held open the bag, I scooped the piles in, and we carried them to the curb.

"You want a beer?" I asked, wiping the sweat from my forehead.

"Okay," Yang said. I went inside and got two cold ones from the fridge, and we sat together, on the splintering cedar of the back deck, watching the sun fall behind the trees and the first stars blink to life above us.

"Can't beat a cold beer," I said, taking a swig.

"Yes," Yang said. He followed my lead and took a long drink. I could hear the liquid sloshing down into his stomach canister.

"This is what men do for the family," I said, gesturing with my beer to the leafless yard. Without realizing it, I had slipped into thinking of Yang as my son, imagining that one day he'd be raking leaves for his own wife and children. It occurred to me then that Yang's time with us was limited. Eventually, he'd be shut down and stored in the basement— an antique that Mika would have no use for when she had children of her own. At that moment I wanted to put my arm around Yang. Instead I said, "I'm glad you came out and worked with me."

"Me, too," Yang said and took another sip of his beer, looking exactly like me in the way he brought the bottle to his lips.

✹

THE KID AT Quick Fix makes me feel much more at ease than Russ. He's wearing a bright red vest with a clean white shirt under it and a name tag that reads HI, I'M RONNIE! The kid's probably not even twenty-one. He's friendly, though, and when I tell him about Yang, he says, "Whoa, that's no good," which is at least a little sympathetic. He tells me they're backed up for an hour. So much for quick, I think. I put Yang on the counter and give my name. "We'll page you once he's ready," Ronnie says.

I spend the time wandering the store. They've got a demo

station of *Championship Boxing,* so I put on the jacket and glasses and take on a guy named Vance, who's playing in California. I can't figure out how to dodge or block though, and when I throw out my hand, my guy on the screen just wipes his nose with his glove. Vance beats the shit out of me, so I put the glasses and vest back on the rack and go look at other equipment. I'm playing with one of the new ThoughtPhones when I hear my name paged over the loudspeaker, so I head back to the Repair counter.

"Fried," the kid tells me. "Honestly, it's probably good he bit it. He's a really outdated model." Ronnie is rocking back and forth on his heels as though impatient to get on to his next job.

"Isn't there anything you can do?" I ask. "He's my daughter's Big Brother."

"The language system is fully functional. If you want, I can separate the head for you."

"Are you kidding? I'm not giving my daughter her brother's head to play with."

"Oh," the kid says. "Well, um, we could remove the voice box for you. And we can recycle the body and give you twenty dollars off any digital camera."

"How much is all this going to cost?"

"It's ninety-five for the checkup, thirty-five for disposal, and voice box removal will be another hundred and fifty. You're probably looking at about three hundred after labor and taxes."

I think about taking him back to Russ, but there's no way. When he'd told me Yang was beyond saving, I gave him a look of distrust that anyone could read loud and clear. "Go ahead and remove the voice box," I say, "but no recycling. I want to keep the body."

※

GEORGE IS OUTSIDE throwing a football around with his identical twins when I pull in. He raises his hand to his kids to stop them from throwing the ball and comes over to the low hedge that separates our driveways. "Hey, how'd it go with Russ?" he asks as I get out of the car.

"Not good." I tell him about Yang, getting a second opinion, how I've got his voice box in the backseat, his body in a large Quick Fix bag in the trunk. I tell him all this with as little emotion as possible. "What can you expect from electronics?" I say, attempting to appear nonchalant.

"Man, I'm really sorry for you," George says, his voice quieter than I've ever heard it. "Yang was a good kid. I remember the day he came over to help Dana carry in the groceries. The kids still talk about that fortune-telling thing he showed them with the three coins."

"Yeah," I say, looking at the bushes. I can feel the tears starting again. "Anyhow, it's no big deal. Don't let me keep you from your game. We'll figure it out." Which is a complete lie. I have no clue how we're going to figure anything out.

We needed Yang, and there's no way we can afford another model.

"Hey, listen," George says. "If you guys need help, let us know. You know, if you need a day sitter or something. I'll talk to Dana—I'm sure she'd be up for taking Mika." George reaches out across the hedge, his large hand coming straight at me. For a moment I flash back to *Championship Boxing* and think he's going to hit me. Instead he pats me on the shoulder. "I'm really sorry, Jim," he says.

✱

THAT NIGHT, I lie with Mika in bed and read her *Goodnight Moon*. It's the first time I've read to her in months. The last time was when we visited Kyra's folks and had to shut Yang down for the weekend. Mika's asleep by the time I reach the last page. I give her a kiss on her head and turn out the lights. Kyra's in bed reading.

"I guess I'm going to start digging now," I say.

"Come here," she says, putting her book down. I cross the room and lie across our bed, my head on her belly.

"Do you miss him, too?" I ask.

"Mm-hm," she says. She puts her hand on my head and runs her fingers through my hair. "I think saying goodbye tomorrow is a good idea. Are you sure it's okay to have him buried out there?"

"Yeah. There's no organic matter in him. The guys at

Quick Fix dumped his stomach canister." I look up at our ceiling, the way our lamp casts a circle of light and then a dark shadow. "I don't know how we're going to make it without him."

"Shhh." Kyra strokes my hair. "We'll figure it out. I spoke with Tina Matthews after you called me today. You remember her daughter, Lauren?"

"The clone?"

"Yes. She's home this semester; college wasn't working for her. Tina said Lauren could watch Mika if we need her to."

I turn my head to look at Kyra. "I thought we didn't want Mika raised by a clone."

"We're doing what we have to do. Besides, Lauren is a nice girl."

"She's got that glassy-eyed apathetic look. She's exactly like her mother," I say. Kyra doesn't say anything. She knows I'm being irrational, and so do I. I sigh. "I just really hoped we could keep clones out of our lives."

"For how long? Your brother and Margaret are planning on cloning this summer. You're going to be an uncle soon enough."

"Yeah," I say quietly.

Ever since I was handed Yang's voice box, time has slowed down. The light of the setting sun had stretched across the wood floors of our home for what seemed an eternity. Sounds have become crisper as well, as though, until now, I'd been living with earplugs. I think about the way Mika's eyelids fluttered as she slept, the feel of George's hand against my arm. I sit up, turn toward Kyra, and kiss her. The softness of her lips makes me remember the first time we kissed. Kyra squeezes my hand. "You better start digging so I can comfort you tonight," she says. I smile and ease myself off the bed. "Don't worry," Kyra says, "it'll be a good funeral."

In the hallway, on my way toward the staircase, the cracked door of Yang's room stops me. Instead of going down, I walk across the carpeting to his door, push it open, and flick on the light switch. There's his bed, perfectly made with the corners tucked in, a writing desk, a heavy oak dresser, and a closet full of black suits. On the wall is a poster of China that Brothers & Sisters Inc. sent us and a pennant from the Tigers game I took Yang to. There's little in the minimalism of his décor to remind me of him. There is, however, a baseball glove on the shelf by his bed. This was a present Yang bought for himself with the small allowance we provided him. We were at Toys"R"Us when Yang placed the glove in the shopping cart. We didn't ask him about it, and he didn't mention why he was buying it. When he came home, he put it on the shelf near his Tigers pennant, and there it sat untouched.

Along the windowsill, Yang's collection of dead moths and butterflies look as though they're ready to take flight. He collected them from beneath our bug zapper during the summer and placed their powdery bodies by the window. I walk over and examine the collection. There's the great winged luna moth, with its two mock eyes staring at me, the mosaic of a monarch's wing, and a collection of smaller nondescript brown and silvery gray moths. Kyra once asked him about his insects. Yang's face illuminated momentarily, the lights beneath his cheeks burning extra brightly, and he'd said, "They're very beautiful, don't you think?" Then, as though suddenly embarrassed, he segued to a Fun Fact regarding the brush-footed butterfly of China.

What arrests me, though, are the objects on his writing desk. Small matchboxes are stacked in a pile on the center of the table, the matchsticks spread across the expanse like tiny logs. In a corner is an orange-capped bottle of Elmer's that I recognize as the one from my toolbox. What was Yang up to? A log cabin? A city of small wooden men and women? Maybe this was Yang's attempt at art—one that, unlike the calligraphy he was programmed to know, was entirely his own. Tomorrow I'll bag his suits, donate them to Goodwill, and throw out the Brothers & Sisters poster, but these match-boxes, the butterflies, and the baseball glove, I'll save. They're the only traces of the boy Yang might have been.

※

THE FUNERAL GOES well. It's a beautiful October day, the sky thin and blue, and the sun lights up the trees, bringing out the ocher and amber of the season. I imagine what the three of us must look like to the neighbors. A bunch of kooks burying their electronic equipment like pagans. I don't care. When I think about Yang being ripped apart in a recycling plant, or stuffing him into our plastic garbage can and setting him out with the trash, I know this is the right decision. Standing together as a family, in the corner of our backyard, I say a couple of parting words. I thank Yang for all the joy he brought to our lives. Then Mika and Kyra say goodbye. Mika begins to cry, and Kyra and I bend down and put our arms around her, and we stay there, holding one another in the early morning sunlight.

When it's all over, we go back inside to have breakfast. We're eating our cereal when the doorbell rings. I get up and answer it. On our doorstep is a glass vase filled with orchids and white lilies. A small card is attached. I kneel down and open it. *Didn't want to disturb you guys. Just wanted to give you these. We're all very sorry for your loss—George, Dana, and the twins.* Amazing, I think. This from a guy who paints his face for Super Bowl games.

"Hey, look what we got," I say, carrying the flowers into the kitchen. "They're from George."

"They're beautiful," Kyra says. "Come, Mika, let's go put those in the living room by your brother's picture." Kyra helps Mika out of her chair, and we walk into the other room together.

It was Kyra's idea to put the voice box behind the photograph. The photo is a picture from our trip to China last summer. In it, Mika and Yang are playing at the gate of a park. Mika stands at the port, holding the two large iron gates together. From the other side, Yang looks through the hole of the gates at the camera. His head is slightly cocked, as though wondering who we all are. He has a placid non-smile/non-frown, the expression we came to identify as Yang at his happiest.

"You can talk to him," I say to Mika as I place the flowers next to the photograph.

"Goodbye, Yang," Mika says.

"Goodbye?" the voice box asks. "But, little sister, where are we going?"

Mika smiles at the sound of her Big Brother's voice, and looks up at me for instruction. It's an awkward moment. I'm not about to tell Yang that the rest of him is buried in the backyard.

"Nowhere," I answer. "We're all here together."

There's a pause as though Yang's thinking about something. Then, quietly, he asks, "Did you know over two million workers died during the building of the Great Wall of China?" Kyra and I exchange a look regarding the odd coincidence of this Fun Fact, but neither of us says anything. Then Yang's voice starts up again. "The Great Wall is over ten thousand *li* long. A *li* is a standardized Chinese unit of measurement that is equivalent to one thousand six hundred and forty feet."

"Wow, that's amazing," Kyra says, and I stand next to her, looking at the flowers George sent, acknowledging how little I truly know about this world.

THE CARTOGRAPHERS

PUBLICLY, WE SOLD memories under Quimbly, Barrett & Woods, but when it was just the three of us, working late into the night, we thought of ourselves as mapmakers. There was something nautical about the loft we'd rented: the massive oak beams and triangular plate glass window that stood like a sail at the end of the room. In the day it revealed the tar-papered roofs of neighboring apartment buildings, and at night framed the illuminated Brooklyn Bridge and Manhattan's skyline. We called it the Crow's Nest, and we were the captains, lording over the memories of the world as we drew our maps into our programs. Here was the ocean, here the ships, here the hotel, here the path that led to town, here the street vendors, here the memories of children we never had and parents much better than the ones we did. And far out there was the edge of the world.

What happens when you get to the edge?

You fall off, we joked.

Early on, there were many edges. They existed within our restaurants and hotels as well as the borders of our cities. Most of our hotel rooms were well charted—open the drawer and you'd find a Bible, take the paintings down and there'd be more wall—but behind the closed doors of neighboring rooms there was nothing but white light. There are, of course, the Japanese maximalists, like the legendary Taka Shimazaki, who design every carpet fiber of every hotel room to avoid any edges, but what Quimbly, Barrett, and I found was that most people trusted memories like they trusted films. You beam a movie between your eyes and remember the plot in vivid detail; you don't wonder where a sidekick's parents live. When you beam a vacation, you remember swimming at the beach and caipirinhas in coconut shells, not the unexplored outskirts of town. Granted, if a tourist tried to remember swimming far enough, say, past the ships, had they gone farther than the edge of town, up a highway, stepped onto the dirt roads at the edge of the map, they'd see that place where the ground ended and the white light began, but people were happy with their memories. What they wanted was a family trip that went well. They wanted the feeling of skydiving to tingle their bones. They didn't care about the rivets and bolts of the plane they jumped from; they merely wanted to remember that the pilot's name was Chip, that he patted them on the back, that he'd said *nice jump.*

What the populace wanted, what they still want, what they'll always want, is pulp cybernetics. Perhaps not so cheap as the corner-store memories China's producing—$8.99 porn thrills so poorly constructed you can see the patches of light where the software burns through the girls' skin—but give them palm trees, a restaurant with an attractive server, coral reefs, and sand dollars for the kids, and you have a package that retails for $79.99.

※

IT WAS SHORTLY after *Circuitry* did the article on us that Quimbly began experimenting with bad memories. It was a natural progression for him. He specialized in emotional recollections: childhoods, marriages, and adolescence. He'd always cringed from anything Hallmarky—the happy marriages and quintessential childhoods—"puppies and kittens" as he called them. His first generation of memories all contained some element of sadness within them: grandchildren for the childless elderly and losses of virginity to lonely men who'd never known love. But there was something truly sinister to Quimbly's second batch. He sold heroin addictions to artists wanting darker aesthetics, affairs to couples who'd never cheated on one another, gunfights to rappers, and suicide attempts to Goth kids.

It was to get away from the dark energies Quimbly was manufacturing that I ended up meeting Cynthia. She was sitting in the coffee shop, across from my office, where I'd go to get coffee, clear my head, and work on constructing happier memories. There was no computer or phone in front of her, only an open journal that she leaned over in concentration. I was fascinated. I hadn't seen anyone using a pen since college, and even then it was mostly older professors who'd used them. She was in her thirties, with long brown hair and flushed cheeks, and every now and again she rested the pen against her bottom lip as she tapped her sandaled foot against the table. If her pen hadn't run dry, she probably never would have seen me.

"Hey," she said.

"Me?" I asked stupidly; there was no one else around.

"Yeah, you. Do you have a pen?" She held hers in the air. "This one's done for."

"Sorry," I said and looked back at my tablet, wishing I wasn't such an idiot around women. Say something, I told myself, and so I looked back up and said, "Hey." She raised her eyes. "I'll go ask if the barista has one."

It turned out he didn't. I walked back to her table. "Sorry," I said, "no luck."

"Doesn't surprise me." She closed her journal.

"What are you writing?"

"Memories," she said, and pointed her pen at my tablet. "What about you?"

"Pretty much the same. It's my work; I make memories. Maybe you've heard of us? Quimbly, Barrett, and Woods?" She shook her head. "We're in a lot of blogs right now."

"I don't read blogs," she said. "I try to stay disconnected."

"You've heard of beamed memories, though, right?" She

shook her head again. "Well, I'm Adam," I said, and extended my hand.

"Cynthia," she said.

"I could show you what I do, if you'd like. Our workshop's just across the street. I'm sure there's a pen there."

She put her journal in her bag. "Sure," she said. "Show me your memories."

※

CYNTHIA KEPT ME out of the office that weekend. It'd been a long time since I'd been with anyone, and never with someone like Cynthia. When we lay in bed together, I could feel the loneliness of my previous life, filled with computer programming and take-out containers, giving way to the happiness of a future together. In short, I was falling in love.

I called in sick Monday and stayed in bed with her, afraid that if I left, she'd disappear. It was the first time in months that I didn't work on constructing memories. Instead, I let my mind fill with details of her: what her lips felt like, the timbre of her voice when she said my name, the way morning spread across the bedroom.

When I finally returned to work on Tuesday and told the guys, I got ribbed by Quimbly. "So that's what happens when you get laid? You stop showing up?" I shrugged and blushed. "Thought you'd both left me," he said. "Barrett's lost in the Bible."

Barrett was sitting by his computer with his head down,

the golden-rimmed pages of a King James on his desk. He'd found his niche with religious experiences. "What are you doing?" I asked him.

"Shhh . . . ," he said darkly, and didn't look up.

"He's writing Sunday sermons now," Quimbly said. "Turns out folks are just as happy thinking they've been to church than actually going. Barrett, put that fucking Bible down, we've got something serious to talk about." Barrett raised a bloodshot glare from the book before marking the page and rising.

We'd gotten our first complaint. A tech-savvy grad student had intentionally gone seeking the edge. He'd tried to remember driving to the border of the Mexican town we'd created for spring break and had run into the white light. His blog posts were already circulating the Internet.

"We haven't been designing tight enough memories," Quimbly said.

"The kid went searching," I said defensively; it'd been my memory. "We can't control where our users go."

"Maybe not, but we can test each other's memories," Quimbly said. "From now on, before we release anything for sale, you go into Barrett's memories, he goes into yours, and both of you go into mine. You test out the edges. Search every alleyway, open every door, drive as far as you can. You find the edge of a memory, you fix it. Go ahead and test at home if you want, just make sure you log every beam."

"And what are you going to do?" I asked.

"I'm the control group," Quimbly said. He promised to watch over us and hold our memories straight. "Don't worry," he said, "I'll keep your brains from getting fried."

※

THE PROBLEM WITH testing memories was that after enough beams, it became impossible to recognize the difference between authentic memories and beamed ones. Had I really fought in Afghanistan? Cynthia was lying next to me in bed, reading a book. It was one of her things—she read actual books. Where she found them, I have no idea. But there she'd be, pillows propped behind her head, reading a novel word by word, page after page, taking endless hours when she could've had the thing memorized in minutes.

"Did I ever fight in Afghanistan?" I asked.

"You weren't born yet," she said dryly.

"How about Bermuda?"

She lowered her book onto her knees and shook her head. "The last place you actually went was your parents' house for Thanksgiving."

It was February. I tried to remember back to November, the dinner with my parents, but it seemed less real than my memories of the tropics. "Are you sure?" I asked.

She raised her book. "Yeah, I'm positive. You've got to stop beaming."

Cynthia was vegan and almost entirely anti-tech. She was devoted to causes like buying back land for Native Americans and safeguarding water rights for third world countries. Though I supported her causes, I resented that she never praised my work. "You know that indigenous tribes are buying our memories, right?"

She let out a heavy sigh. "I'm not trying to put down your work," she said. "But you're spending more time trying to figure out memories you never had than making real memories with me. You're getting addicted."

This wasn't entirely true. In those first months together, I'd go to the Crow's Nest and work on memories during the day, then take nights off with her. A bistro had opened near my place, and we'd go there on the weekends for breakfast. Nights we'd order in Chinese, lie in bed, and make love. But Cynthia was right. There were many times when she'd catch me staring out the window, trying to find the edge of Quimbly's latest memory.

At work, Quimbly, Barrett, and I focused on making our memories last longer. The key was to package memories together. A vacation to Europe couldn't simply be the Eiffel Tower and the Louvre; it needed to involve the airplane ride, the week at work before, the mundane details that helped make the memories stick.

"All good memories have boredom buried in them," Quimbly told us one night.

"You should write children's books," I said.

Barrett was unusually quiet. He'd grown more silent ever since he began designing past-life memories, and we mistook his silence for Zen satori rather than the madness that was slowly taking his mind.

"Look, if we make perfect memories, we're not going to have customers left," Quimbly said and leaned over the coffee table. "The key to our success is to give people ninety-nine percent perfect experiences. Make them *almost* happy, and they'll keep buying. Trust me on this." Then he gave us the next batch of memories to test.

※

CYNTHIA HATED QUIMBLY from the first time they met. I'd invited Quimbly for dinner in hopes that they'd get along, but by the time we sat down to eat, it was a mess. Cynthia was working on a clean-water project for children in Mali and, in typical Quimbly fashion, he started an argument. "Look, I get you, it's good to give them water, but let's be honest, water's not going to save them. They're going to die from disease, civil war, malnutrition. Give them memory sticks and at least they'll have happy memories before they die."

"That's really sick," Cynthia said.

"You're telling me if you could give them a happy childhood, you'd deny them?"

"It's not a happy childhood; it's forgetting their actual past."

"I think you *want* them to suffer," Quimbly said. "Somehow their pain makes things real for you."

I tried to soothe the tension, suggested we do both, send

them water *and* memories. Getting the kids water made sense, I said, it was the right thing to do, but I didn't see any harm in giving kids good memories as well.

"Fuck that," Cynthia said. "What you're talking about is making a bunch of beam-heads who won't ever work for social change."

"That's not true," I said. "We're designing parents for inner-city kids with horrible upbringings; we've donated memories to the poor."

"That's not social change," Cynthia said and got up from the table, leaving her dinner unfinished. "I hope you guys know that the work you're doing is evil."

Quimbly took a sip of wine and gave me a smile after she left the room. "You sure she's the one?" he asked. "You might want to take a closer look there, buddy." He stayed long enough to finish his dinner and fix himself another drink, and then, when I said it was probably best I see him tomorrow, he left. I cleared the dishes from the table and went into the bedroom, where Cynthia sat reading.

"I can't believe you work with that asshole."

"You guys didn't get off to the best start," I admitted. "He's actually a good guy; he just likes to push people's buttons. He's a brilliant designer."

"That kind of brilliance I can do without." She looked at me for the first time since I'd entered the room. "His fetish is getting inside people's heads. That's why he likes being, what did you call it, the 'control group'? Control freak is more like it. He loves that he controls your memories—you're his guinea pigs."

In retrospect, I can see that this was precisely what Quimbly was doing. I'd thought of him as a friend—and maybe Barrett and I were as close to friends as Quimbly would ever be capable of—but deep down, we were just social experiments to him. I couldn't see it then, though, and was angry at Cynthia for calling our work evil and me a guinea pig.

"It's no different than what you do," I said before I could stop myself. "You only want *real* memories based on *your* plans for us. You talk about a farmhouse that doesn't even exist yet. You want to create my memories as much as he does."

She looked at me for a moment before turning back to her book. "You don't have a fucking clue what you're talking about."

"Right," I said. "That's why I have a company worth millions, and you're just reading a book."

"Here," she said, tossing me a pillow. "How about we sleep apart tonight."

And so I went back into the living room and lay on the couch, late into the night, wondering why I'd defended Quimbly against the woman who loved me. Perhaps this proved everything Cynthia was trying to tell me—that he'd already gotten so deeply into my head that I'd willingly hurt anyone who reminded me, not out of control but out of love, that I'd never been to Russia or had a brother. It was this thought that brought me back to the bedroom, to climb beneath the sheets and to hold her, telling her I was sorry and that I wanted to make memories together.

IT WAS HARD to shake the memory of our first real fight. In the months that followed, Cynthia and I avoided that night with Quimbly, and I made an effort to be more present. We went for walks, ate at our favorite bistro, and we'd return to my apartment and make love. But there was a growing distance between us, and when she'd fall asleep, I'd edge my way out of bed to beam high-end memories in the darkness of our bathroom. It was, I realize now, a time when I had everything: a woman who loved me, a company worth millions, and bidders waiting in line to buy us out. Quimbly was calling us the history-makers. It was a time when I believed we would become the masters of the world. Then we destroyed it all.

"We'll make a fortune," Quimbly said, putting his palms together.

"What exactly are you suggesting?" I asked.

"Simple ad placement. We layer one into your Cuba memory. Show sweat beading along a glass of Coke, carbonation fizzing. We're talking big money for a single placement."

Barrett was deadly silent. Over the past weeks he'd become increasingly taciturn, but this was something different. His lips were working back and forth against each other as though he was grinding his teeth.

"We're selling out?" I asked.

"Just being practical. They're lining up at our door. We could own the world."

"*Enough!*" Barrett ordered, his voice echoing in the beams.

"Hold on," Quimbly said. "You haven't heard me out."

"*You dare argue with me?*" Barrett boomed, his fingers clenching. "Do you know who I am? I am the Lord of lords and the King of kings; I am the alpha and omega; I am the Lord Supreme." He rose from his seat, stepping onto the couch and lifting his hands into the air as though holding a staff. "You, who sow discontent, shall be crucified! Your hands and feet shall be cut off—"

"Barrett, chill," Quimbly said.

"In my presence the mountains quake! The hills melt, the earth trembles, its people are destroyed! The day of judgment has come!" Then Barrett jumped from the couch and seized Quimbly around the neck so hard it left bruises for weeks after. It was when I saw Quimbly's face turning blue that I took my beer bottle and broke it over Barrett's head. We tied his legs and arms together and called 911.

That was the end of Barrett. He was sent upstate, where he ranted at the walls and played God to anyone willing to listen. When we cleaned out his apartment, we discovered the memories he'd never told us about. He'd begun a personal log, which detailed beaming thousands of his own created memories, the notebook deteriorating into pages of an indecipherable alphabet.

Still, Barrett had tried, in his own way, to warn us. Come

May, less than a week after our first memory ads launched, the word spread that we'd sold out. A blogger posted a scathing piece that went viral. Memory start-ups took the bait and began selling their memories as "100% ad free."

"Who'd have guessed they'd resent having their brain space tweaked, they never seemed to mind before," Quimbly joked. But he, too, was shaken. Within the month, sales fell and our inboxes were full of hate mail. We were no longer the masters of the universe, just owners of a failing company.

※

QUIMBLY ENDED UP taking a job for another company that manufactured thought ads. He told me the news as we cleared the Crow's Nest of our belongings, and I listened vaguely as I cleaned out my desk, realizing the life we'd created together was now only a memory. Barrett was gone, Quimbly was moving on, and I had nothing but my dwindling savings and Cynthia.

"People resist thought ads, but soon enough they'll be as commonplace as napkins," he said. "I can get you in, but first clean yourself up."

I looked up from the floorboards where I'd been staring, thinking about the years I'd spent in the war. "What do you mean 'clean myself up'?"

"How many memories are you beaming a day?"

"Not that many," I lied. Like Barrett, I was designing my own memories and downloading them when I couldn't sleep.

I still logged the memories I tested, but not my late-night binges or the hundreds of high-end Shimazaki memories I'd spent my bank account on. "Maybe a few a day," I said.

"Uh-huh. Look, I'm not telling you what to do with your life, but you're starting to act like Barrett. Go visit him. Refresh your memory of what happens when you lose track."

"I'm fine," I said.

"No, you're not," Quimbly said. "You probably don't even remember the time we went skiing."

"Of course I do: Breckenridge, three days of fresh powder."

Quimbly shook his head. "That was one of mine," he said. "Listen, I know you won't stop beaming because I tell you to, but if you're going to keep beaming, at least use this one next." Quimbly pulled a memory stick from his pocket. "It's a going-away present."

"Thanks," I said, and though I knew he and Cynthia were right, and that the best thing for me would be never to touch another memory again, I couldn't help myself from reaching out and taking the gift.

When I got back to the apartment, I left the boxes from the office in the hallway and sat down on the couch. I placed the tip of Quimbly's memory stick against my forehead and pressed the button. I was halfway into the beam when Cynthia walked in.

"You've got to be fucking kidding me," she said.

"What?" I opened my eyes.

"You just went bankrupt because of those things and

you're—" Then she stopped. "No, you know what—go ahead and enjoy yourself, beam all night if you want. I'm out of here." She raised her two fingers in a peace sign, then turned her back on me and left the room.

"Hey!" I said. "Just wait a minute, I'm almost done." I finished Quimbly's gift and got up to find her, but she wasn't anywhere. Not in the bedroom, the kitchen, or the bathroom. The only trace of her was a note taped to the mirror. *I'm done. Goodbye, Adam. Thanks for the memories. Sorry you liked yours better.*

For the next two weeks I binged on memories to keep from letting the pain sink in. I went to the Himalayas and gambled in Vegas, I slept with porn stars and got wasted with celebrities, I drove in stretch limos through Hollywood and sat on the beaches of the world watching sunrise after tropical sunrise, beaming one after another memory, until one morning I found myself in the early light, dehydrated, shaking and sweaty, without a clue of who I was.

Did I have parents? Were they both still alive?

In one memory I recalled attending their funeral. In another I pictured them tanned and happy in L.A. And in yet another I remembered our childhood home in Tibet. I scrolled through my phone, my grip sweaty and slippery, until I found a number listed as *Home.*

A woman picked up on the third ring.

"Hello?" she said, her voice distant and unfamiliar.

"Mom?" I asked. "Can I come home?"

❊

MY LIFE SINCE leaving the memory business has mostly been recovery and learning to forgive Quimbly. I work to get my memories straight. I'll recall my parents' death, envision myself as an angry teenager, smoking cigarettes in the Rockies after their funeral. Then I'll hear the floor squeak above me, hear my mother in the kitchen, listen to my father cough before he lets the door slam, and I'll remember that I never lived in Colorado but grew up here in Brooklyn. I live in my parents' basement again, like when I was a teenager, and I never smoked cigarettes, merely spent my daylight hours in this subterranean darkness programming computers.

I got a job at a coffee shop in the neighborhood, where I help curate the art on the walls and brew lattes for the kids who've settled this outpost of New York City. And I work on my letter to Cynthia. I sit, pen in hand, trying to remember what love felt like. *I miss you,* I write. *I'm better now. I want to make real memories together.*

Quimbly saved me, there's no doubt about that. Had I never fallen in love with Cynthia, she never could've left me; had she never left me, I never would've stopped beaming. Typical, though, that even Quimbly's acts of kindness were sadistic. It was when I'd finished my letter that I finally understood what his going-away present had been. After sealing my pages into the envelope, I picked up my pen to write Cynthia's address, and had no clue where she lived. Every memory I had of her involved my apartment, the bistro, or walking the streets in winter. Hadn't I ever seen her apartment, I wondered. And then, before I could stop myself, I realized I'd found the edge. Light poured through the cracks where stories of her family should've been. It came streaming in from the hallway of my old apartment, which had never been clean, but was a dark, curtained cave filled with take-out containers and an unmade bed. The bistro where we ate never had a name; the Chinese takeout never had fortune cookies. And yet, all the other details had been masterfully placed by Quimbly, every memory bunched together to form a life that had never happened. I sat there in the coffee shop, the light fluttering behind my eyelids, feeling my heart sail off the edge of the world.

Love scars memories, even if it was never real. When I walk the streets I think: we walked here together, she used to touch my arm like this, and the pain of white emptiness sets in. You can't get rid of memories; you can only try to ignore them. I've been weeding through my old memories, finding the edge of the world in one memory after another. I was never in France or Tokyo, have never seen the California redwoods or swum in the Caribbean, and I've never made love with Cynthia. All the same, I keep working on my letters to her. I tell her I can still remember her skin against mine as we slept, the light in her eyes when I'd open my apartment door for her, and the sound of her voice, telling me, over and over, just how much she loved me.

HEARTLAND

MY SON IS doing fantastic until the elimination round. Then he gets to the quiz questions and I watch him fall apart. His little face goes tight, the way it does near a barking dog, and he starts haphazardly punching the buzzer—not even listening to the questions. For a moment I want to bury my face in my hands, almost do, but then I realize it'd be me and not one of the other usual schmucks on TV crying. So I sit up straight and keep my eyes on Sam, trying to look supportive as I watch him lose ten thousand bucks.

There are papers to sign and hands to shake when the show is over, and then we're driving home. Sam's strapped into his booster seat with the *Scaredy Cat: Home Version* game in his lap. By now it's dark. Only 6 P.M., but Indiana's late October light is long gone. I hold both hands on the steering wheel and stare out at the headlights of the opposite lanes and the blackness of the clay fields around us.

Sam was a beautiful baby, which is what helped us land

him the diaper ads, but ever since he turned seven he's become a normal kid. *Scaredy Cat* was his one big shot. The winner of the show always lands a TV ad, sometimes even an appearance on KidMTV. That's how Mindy Sands got so big. But that's never going to happen to Sam. He doesn't even know how to play an instrument.

Sam's been quiet the whole ride. He can feel when I'm upset. Finally he speaks, his voice small from the backseat. "Daddy, are you angry?"

"No," I say.

"I thought I knew the answers."

"Yeah, I know," and before I can stop myself I add, "but you've got to listen to the questions."

"I know. I'm sorry."

"I mean, you weren't even listening to the questions. You were just hitting the buttons."

"I was trying to listen. . . . I mean, I was . . . well, I mean . . ."

Then there's just silence. I look in the rearview mirror to see Sam staring out his window, tears falling down his cheeks. "It's okay," I say. It's too late, though. The darkness of the backseat is broken only by the passing bands of light from the overhead streetlights. In those momentary flashes I can see he's still staring out the window, crying.

I let out a deep sigh. "It's okay, Sam," I say again. "You did the best you could." Then I put on my signal and head for the exit, where I'll find a place to pull over and give him a hug.

※

AT HOME CARA hasn't started dinner yet. She's got Laurie in the crib, where she's gumming the corner of my old iPhone. Cara's at the computer, uploading photos of our furniture and Sam's older toys on e-auction. "Hey," she says, clicking the screen onto her feed when Sam runs into the room. "I saw you on TV, little man."

"Sorry," Sam says.

"Don't be sorry, you were great. Was it gross to eat worms?"

Sam smiles. "Kinda. Sorta like spaghetti that kept wiggling."

"Ew!" she says, scrunching her nose, and gives him a hug. Over his shoulder she mouths to me, *other room.*

"Come on, Sam, let's go make some funny home videos," I say, so Cara can finish uploading the photos.

"All right," Sam says.

We do a couple classic knock-down gags in his bedroom: Sam standing on his tippy toes, trying to hit the light switch and falling back onto his ass, Sam jumping on the bed and falling off the edge. Decent stuff that probably won't make the cut. As a reward, I let him play VirtuCube.

Cara's still on the computer when I walk into the living room.

"Dinner?" I ask.

"Laurie *just* stopped crying and I've been nursing for the past hour. Let's order in pizza."

I feel the familiar flush of irritation beneath my skin. "I was hoping you'd cook for us."

"Yeah, and I was hoping you'd prepped Sam better for the quiz questions."

"Thanks, you've got a real gift for compassion." I walk into the kitchen to get a beer. Cara's up from her chair, following me. I open the fridge and take a Corona.

"I thought you were quitting."

That was our deal. She would quit coffee; I'd quit drinking. I pop the bottle with a lighter and toss the cap into the garbage under the sink, where we keep our bucket of compost. A swarm of fruit flies is buzzing in the murky darkness of sponges and Brillo pads. "Can't you at least take out the compost?" I say.

Laurie starts crying from the other room. Cara looks at me. "It's your turn to take her."

"Fine, I'll take her *and* the compost out."

I put my beer on the counter and sweep Laurie from the crib. I turn her so she's facing me, then go into the kitchen and crouch to get the bucket. Laurie begins to cry again.

"Give me her," Cara says.

"I've got her."

"She's not happy with how you're holding her. Give her

to me." Cara puts her hands around Laurie and pulls her away. I'm left with the bucket of compost and the fruit flies. I take the compost, step outside, and slam the door behind me.

What's left of our yard is a mess from yesterday's rain. Ever since we sold off the topsoil, the clay makes walking treacherous. It's the same for every yard in our neighborhood. I put on muck boots and climb down the makeshift steps that Heartland Gardens put in when they carted our soil away; then I slog through the slippery clay to the corner of our yard where we're trying to make dirt. Blackened banana peels, old coffee grounds, and moldy vegetables sit in the wired-off compost pile. At this rate we'll have usable soil in a decade.

I hear Laurie still wailing inside. She's been wailing since she came into the world. Laurie was born with a stray eye. Minor corrective surgery would've fixed it, except minor corrective surgery when you're not covered means no minor corrective surgery. Which meant no baby commercials for Laurie.

I crouch down next to the compost and look up at the sky, which is covered by gray clouds. Seems like it rains every day now. When I was a kid, we used to have these long beautiful Indiana summers. Now we just have a drawn-out rainy fall— all year long. With the soil gone, it turns our backyards into clay pits. The clay runs off onto the streets, where it hardens between rains until the city comes and sprays the sludge into the sewers. I look at the telephone and electric wires cutting across our patch of sky, feeling like the whole world is coming down around me.

Cara is nursing Laurie when I come back in. I lean over the chair and give her a kiss. "Sorry," I say. "I just don't know what we're going to do."

"I know," she says. Her skin smells like apricot, a familiar smell that I'd somehow forgotten, and for a moment I feel our closeness. "Did you remember to take out the recycling?" she says.

The moment is gone. I force myself not to say anything. I'll just be an asshole, she'll get angry, Sam will see us fighting, and we'll all be miserable. I can't go there. Not tonight. I take out my wallet and put a twenty by the computer.

"What's this for?"

"Pizza for you and Sam."

"Huh?" she says and looks at me.

I go into the kitchen and finish what's left of my beer. Then I put the empty bottle in our recycling bin, overflowing with bottles of biodegradable dish soap and empty cans of beans. "I'm going out," I say.

"*Going out?* I've been taking care of Laurie all day."

"Sorry," I say. "I need some time alone." I tote the recycling past her, through the living room to the front door.

"What about me? You ever consider I need a break, too?"

I'm already out the door, closing it behind me. By the time I get to the curb, I imagine she's going to be in the doorway yelling at me for the entire neighborhood to hear. Not that it matters. Most of the houses have been empty for years. The only houses with signs of life are at the end of the cul-de-sac, where blue recycling bins have been set out in the mud. But Cara doesn't come out. Not by the time I've separated the cardboard from plastics, not by the time I've gotten to the car and unlocked it, not even when I pull out of our driveway and leave.

❋

THE SHOVEL IS located down 37, just north of Martinsville. It's fashioned to look like the interior of a potting shed, a real note of irony for all of us who no longer have our yards. The walls sport fake bags of potting soil, shovels, hoes, chicken wire, and dirt-stained terra-cotta pots. Jim's sitting at the bar, waiting for me with a pitcher of stout in front of him. He's my only friend left from the old job.

"Tough night, huh?" he says, filling a pint glass and pushing it in front of me.

"Every time I think I'm going to quit drinking, the fighting starts up again. That's all we do now: fight, fuck, make up, then do it again."

"At least you're fucking," Jim says and lifts his glass. "Here's to quitting."

We clink and I take a sip. There's the familiar tang of alcohol against the tongue, the molasses sweetness of the stout. *Dream Girls* is on the flat-screen over the bar. One of the frumpy wives has undergone reconstructive surgery to appear identical to her husband's favorite movie star.

"I just don't know what's wrong with us," I say. "We used to have it good together. Now it's like we're not even a couple. I come home, I want to be with her, and she just hands me the baby. She thinks I'm an asshole. Maybe I am. Tell me the truth: I sound like an asshole, right?"

"Nah," Jim says and takes a sip of his beer. "You just need a job, that's all. And you've got to learn to swallow your pride."

Which is true. One of the things I like about Jim is that he's not sentimental. I overthink things. Jim watches shows like *Dream Girls* and doesn't give a shit. "How are things at work?" I ask. "Same crew?"

"More or less. The kid who got hired after you got canned yesterday. Larry caught him stealing topsoil. Had his trunk filled with it."

"What a stupid way to go," I say and realize we're both thinking the same thing. "You know, I was just standing up for my family."

"Forget it," Jim says, looking down at his glass. "It's history."

"What would you have done? Just smile at him and take it?"

"Don't know what I'd have done, but I sure as hell wouldn't have hit the boss," Jim says. Then he turns his eyes back to the TV. On the screen, the husband is making out with his reconstructed wife.

Jim's answer is more or less the same one Cara gave me when I told her what had happened. There had been a car issue that day; Cara needed it, so she dropped me off at work. Sam and Laurie were in the backseat. Larry had been out front, straightening lawn displays, and had seen Laurie. On my way inside to clock in he'd joked, "I think your baby girl was giving me the stink eye."

"What did you say?" I asked, turning to face him across the small square of lawn.

"Hey now, don't you start looking at me cockeyed, too," he said. That's when I hit him. There was no conscious decision about it—just this surge of heat and a streak of green beneath me. Then he was flat on his back and I was on top of him, driving my fist into his face. Jim said I was lucky I only lost my job. Cara said I was a fucking idiot. Which I guess was true, because we were already behind on our second mortgage. Still, it was one of the few things I can remember doing in the past couple years that I actually felt good about.

"You think there's any way I can get back delivering?" I ask.

"Not a fucking chance. You're blacklisted from Fort Wayne to Bedford."

"It's been over a year."

"People remember. Only way you're gonna get a job installing gardens is to move."

"How am I going to do that? I can't sell our house in this market. We're lucky we still have it. You've seen Downtown Indy—tent city."

"That's what I'm saying, *move*. Leave it all behind. Start fresh."

"Move where? Michigan? Illinois? They're all sheets of clay." Jim doesn't answer. "You know, I thought we were going to have a break today. Sam was on—"

"Yeah, Fran told me what happened," Jim says. "Real sorry to hear it. Here, let me fill you up." Jim pours the rest of the pitcher into my glass. "You know, there are still some jobs in Kentucky—they've got patches down there. South America's got some green, places in Brazil—"

"Brazil's finished."

"So try something new, switch professions."

"And do what? Nobody's hiring. Do you know how long the list is to even get a job at *this place*?" I say, tapping the bar.

Above us, *Dream Girls* is finished and the news has come on. It's day nine hundred of the oil spill. There's a picture of the Pacific Ocean, black as soil, followed by photos of obsidian waves crashing against the California coastline. Hawaii is on fire. A company spokesman is standing on a freighter, saying he believes they'll be able to cap the underwater well by July of next year.

"God," I say. "This is really the end, isn't it?"

"Nah," Jim says. "People have been saying the world's gonna end for years. It never does."

"Yeah, but look at that." I point to the screen with my glass. "The land's gone, the water's going. The Northeast doesn't even have decent drinking water anymore. We're done for."

"That's just how it feels 'cause you're in the dumps. Fran and I still got it good. Plenty of people still got it good."

"Yeah, well, we don't have it good," I say, looking into what's left of my pint. The alcohol is hitting me now, dragging me downward. My brain feels like it's full of dirt. "I think we're going to lose the house by Christmas." Above us are rolling photos of the earthquakes in Chile, followed by the recent floods in Japan. I take a long swallow of beer.

"Listen," Jim says, "Fran and I were in a rough spot last spring. Nothing too serious, but cell phone, Internet, cable, 24/7 GPS, online gambling, those kinda things add up. . . ." He takes a sip of his beer and lowers his voice. "You know, you've got a couple of good-looking kids. Really good-looking kids. You ever consider putting photos online?"

I grimace as though my drink's rancid.

"Don't give me that look," Jim says.

I empty my pint glass, put it down on the counter, and face Jim, looking him square in the eyes. "There's no fucking way I'm selling my kids' photos to porn."

"I'm not talking porn," Jim says, "just pictures of them in the bathtub, Cara changing her diaper. Mild stuff, practically family photos. No big deal. Look, it wasn't my first choice either, but I know a guy—completely confidential—you email him the attachments, he sends you a check. You don't have to have any contact with his clients. Two hundred full frontal for boys, three hundred for girls. You get a shot of them together, he'd probably pay six."

"I'm not putting naked photos of my kids out there."

"Who's it hurting? So a couple perverts are willing to pay good money to see them—so what? We're talking a lot of money for a few snapshots. Sure, it's not what anybody wants to do—I didn't want to do it—but it got us through a tough spot. Look, nobody's gonna see the photos except whoever he sells them to. And I'll tell you something, the market will be flooded before you know it. A year from now, those pictures will be buried in the Internet. You need money—this is where the money is."

"I'm not interested," I say.

"Okay, so you're not interested now, but at least let me give you his email in case you change your mind." Jim writes the address down on a napkin and shoves it in my shirt pocket.

"I'm throwing it out," I tell him.

"Do what you need to do," Jim says. "As for me, I'm treating us to another pitcher." Which is kind of him and, though I ought to pay, I just nod my head and say thanks.

REALLY, I SHOULDN'T be driving, and for this reason I take the long back road home, up old 37. Out here on the forgotten highway, I'm alone in the darkness watching my high beams cut across the land and the great pits. Twenty years ago it was all cornfields out here—Indiana soil so rich you could put anything in the dirt and it would grow. Then the companies came for the soil, followed by the clay, and finally the bedrock. All that's left are these pits, abandoned and sinking. They talked for a while of filling the canyons with water, turning the place into a second series of great lakes— private ponds for the rich to float their sailboats on and their children to Jet Ski across. Then the rich moved on—away from this endless stretch of exposed rock and dead earth. Maybe years from now, when we're all gone, some new creature will step forth on these canyons and gaze out at the abyss, never knowing there were once cornfields here.

The rains have started again. The drops splatter against the windshield and make the roads muddy. At one point the mud gets so bad the wipers can't cut it, and I have to pull over to the side of the road. I park beside the tall chain-link fence that separates the state road from the pits. I pop the trunk and take the squeegee from the back. The rain feels good against my skin, sobering, and I take my time, running the rubber blade against the glass and flicking the mud onto the road. Across from the pits, all the foreclosed houses are abandoned. The empty sockets of front yards, yanked from the ground like teeth, are filled with rain. It's kind of beautiful in the darkness, as though the neighborhood is floating. Soon it will be dawn and everything will be ugly, but for now there's an eerie radiance to the world. Perhaps it will be okay, I think. The earth will recover; the world won't ever truly end. Perhaps it will be green again someday. I put the squeegee back in the trunk and start on the road toward home.

There's a story I would like to tell to my children. In this story a boy meets a girl and they fall in love. They both have good jobs and enough money to buy a nice house with acres of land. There are old trees on their land—apples and pears, cherries and plums, blueberry bushes and grapevines. In the late fall, the grass gets sticky with the pulp of fallen fruit, and bees buzz amid the fermenting cores. The family makes pies, and the children's fingers get stained from the blueberries, a light purple hue that remains even after their baths that night. In this home the parents love each other. Sometimes the children see their parents kiss and they feel embarrassed. They are good children, healthy and happy. They ride bicycles with other kids; they grow up, fall in love, and have children of their own who they bring back to the land. And at night, when the moon rises full above their home, the family goes to sleep to the sound of crickets chirping in the high grass.

In this story there is no car pulling into the driveway at 4 A.M., there is no father stumbling to the door as he struggles to find his keys. In this story, when the father goes into his son's room to make sure he's sleeping, he kisses the small boy on his forehead and tucks the blankets up beneath his son's chin, never considering, not even for a moment, rolling the blankets down past the boy's small chest, which rises and falls with every breath, where deep inside there's a heart that loves his father and trusts he will protect him against the monsters of this world.

EXCERPTS FROM
The New World Authorized Dictionary

brainflea *n.* Useless data sent via Brain/Web interface, primarily concerned with the dissemination of product information.

> **2026 Oct 12** Glade Dunning, *Cyberspeak* [posting on think-the-stream], http://www.thinkthestream.com/blog/2026/10/12: Braintwitters started arriving at Podmarket Promos on Saturday afternoon. I was the first to get a complaint, but we were all getting them soon enough. Seemed our latest *brainflea* had sunk in its teeth and wasn't letting go—a particularly viral promo Quimbly dreamed up for BellyBurners that projected itself into the upper right occipital quadrant beneath the eyelid, making it distracting to anyone's vision and ensuring there was no way you were going to blink that one out of your eye.

2027 Feb 1 javinflav on Scooberwatch, http://scooberwatch .com/2027/brainflea-promoz-newzshizzle/#comment -19837: Even with the case of EDs [Extra-invasive Data] like what Podmarket is putting out, the problem with brainfleas is that they're essentially just a retinal base without any deeper ocular invasiveness. If brainfleas can't create a deeper neural probe to leave some sort of ocular trace, you're just going to have people dumping these QBFs [Quick BrainFiles] from their memory (unlike Nerve-Ending-Strings that cling to spinal-receptors, check out Wildgirlz NES#1a-5). That's a lot of eye-space lost for a single brainflea getting squashed in a blink.

mush *v.* ["Just Mush the Bitch," song by American musician, G-Spot] **1.** Heterosexual intercourse wherein the female has her face pressed firmly against a surface (usually floor) in a forceful manner.

2023 Feb 1 G-Spot, http://www.songlyrics/mushthebitch _0985.php: If your girl is acting the slut, just mush the bitch, just mush the bitch / and if the young thing starts acting up, just mush that shit, yeah, mush that shit / I want to see those panties drop / I want to see that cherry pop / as I mush your shit, yeah, mush that shit.

2023 Feb 24 *Late Night with Dymon Shields* (transcript): Dymon Shields: "G-Spot, I think we all want to know, just what is mushing?" G-Spot: "Psh, I'll mush you right now [laughter]. Serious? Well, mushing is when you take your girl and put her face down, you know, against the carpeting or her mom's ratty old bathroom tiles. You know you've been mushing when you can count the tiles on her face when she gets up [laughter]."

2023 March 14 Tommy Tanzotti, *MTV Spring Break Unchained with Tommy Tanzotti* (transcript): "Wassup-wassup? Ohhhh yeah, we here chillin' with the hottest fe-males in Abu Dhabi. Yo, what's your name?" / "Sarah." / "And where you from?" / "I'm from Ohio. I go to Oberlin." / "I bet you do a lot of mushing at Oberlin." / "I sure do." / "Why don't you put your face on the ground and show us how you mush it. Yeah, that's it. Mush it, baby, mush it."

2. To embarrass someone publicly through domination or degradation, often in business.

2024 June 18 Larry Spence, *Business Week:* "When it comes to foreclosing, a lot of us will refer to it as mushing. At the office it's not difficult to hear a quote like, 'You should've seen how I mushed the Johnsons today, had the husband face down, wife crying.'"

orange blossom, orange-blossom *n.* [*THRRADS* 4.b. "A special-purpose high-explosive bomb of incredible damage."

2024] Large and powerful conventional bomb dropped from VICA [*VirtuCube-Interactive-Controlled Aircraft*].

2025 Oct 15 Tim Penicaud, *Military Journal VII,* http://globalsecurity.org/military/mil-0475-usmco.html, TACTICAL SUPPORT FOR AREA "PRAYING MANTIS": The KLMT-8 bomb, which scorches targets with a burst of white phosphorous powder burning at 6700C, was released for use against Turkey. The bomb, also known as an orange-blossom, is able to "liquidate largely populated areas." From an aerial view, each bomb creates a large white starlike pattern that resembles the flower.

2026 Aug 1 Sgt. Nicholas Wobido, *ArmySpeak*: "You try telling my guys we're in a financial squeeze. Men who served with me were torched by orange-blossoms, and we're getting this for our service? I don't know what Washington's thinking, but it's damn clear we've been cut off from medical coverage thanks to it [the Wartime Recuperation Act]."

2026 Oct 17 Tyler Studds, *Entertainment Weekly*: Filming of the comedy, *Duty Calls,* came to an unexpected halt in the capital city of Ankara yesterday when an orange-blossom exploded a little too close for comfort. The reverberations ruffled even the coolheaded indie director, who stood in cargo shorts while dialing in a call to local officials. "Sometimes you just hope they remember we're filming here," he commented to reporters.

tog, TOG, togging [*t*herapy *o*n the *g*o, therapy+jog] *v.* also *n.* The practice of relying upon ITPs (Inner-Ear Therapy Programs) while in a public space, often in the company of others or during social interaction (eating, walking, while in conversation).

2028 March 20 Abercrombie Jones, *Modern Business:* Inner-Ear and AT&T's recent merger means good news for stockholders and good news for customers. Reports show a 12 percent increase in Inner-Ear surgery since the merger went public, and already airports and restaurants are filled with the sound of patrons togging aloud in between IT support and mojitos. Yet, while many users attest to the value of togging, continual wireless therapy does not necessarily equate with balanced lives. Dr. Peter Christoff, Professor of Social-Cybernetics at Johns Hopkins, notes, "A lot of togging can actually lead to a form of social myopia. We've seen these people: the mother togging on parenting while her children are crying, the date who excuses himself to tog romance tips. I think we're going to see an overall increase of chronic togging in the near future."

togger *n.* A person who relies upon ITPs while in public.

> **2028 May 1** Ms. Kathy McGee, *Kathy'sFunPage,* http://
> www.kathysfunpage.com/21994: Well, I'm sure all of you
> are as fed up as me with togging. Yesterday, once again (!),
> I almost flirted with one of these toggers—a real cutie, too,
> in a Sacchi & Tucchi Kevlar helmet. I heard him say, "I
> have a lot of trouble knowing how to speak to women."
> So I turned to him and said, "Why don't you just say
> hello," but he wasn't paying any attention to me; togging
> away as usual. Ugh! When are we going to get some men
> who don't need therapy 24/7!?

> **2028 Dec 20** Aquiles LaGrave, *The Guardian* (London):
> Good news for anyone suffering from togging-fatigue: the
> latest is www.toggerhealing.com, an online social network
> where chronic toggers can connect with other toggers to
> receive therapeutic support from a virtual togging com-
> munity.

urban outfitting *v.* To use discarded materials in order to
increase the safety of a military uniform (see Trash-Fitting
"ATNW" AS 80[2025]: 311-12)

> **2025 Nov 1** Mitsubishi Mikado, *The Philadelphia Reporter:*
> Republican Senator Ed Brendell voiced his objection to
> the Geary Bill, stating that the $187 million proposed for

phosphorous-protective clothing would be better used on an increase of orange-blossoms and other military equipment. "There's no need to upgrade protective equipment," Brendell said. "These guys [soldiers] know how to use the materials they've got to protect themselves. They call it *urban outfitting.*"

2026 Jan 4 Obituaries, *Columbus Informer:* The family of Sgt. David Brown, 19, of Gahanna, learned he was killed Wednesday when an undetonated orange-blossom was used against U.S. forces outside of Istanbul. His parents claim the death could have been prevented. "You can't expect urban outfitting to protect our children against the type of bombs they're using over there," his father said.

2. *n.* Civilian clothing that has been altered by adding protective equipment used by police or military.

2026 May 4 *HipHopJunkyz:* G-Spot most surely got the most style—what with his latest urban outfitting. Those of you who caught his *DeathStarGangsta* tour saw him wearing his M.O.L.L.E. II Bulletproof Carrier Vest and Green Phantom Combat goggles (available at www .downtoparty.com).

2026 August 14 Sandy Sheener, *V Women's Style:* Sacchi & Tucchi released its new fall line of Urban Outfitting in

Copenhagen during last month's fashion week. Bianca wore a Remploy Textile full NBC bodysuit with respirator and gloves, while Kate Swiss wowed the crowd, showing off S&T's latest White Phosphorous line.

wink, winking, Wink *v.* [from *Winker:* social-networking Brain/Web interface site created in 2027 by MIT student Jeremiah Jones, originally called *Socialwinker*] To include or exclude people in your field of vision or hearing by use of *Winker's Blue-Eye®* technology.

2027 Dec 1 Axe Brockman, *StudentSpeak,* Harvard University Press: "We use it at parties, you know, to find out where our friends be at. You turn on Winker and suddenly everyone shuts up and disappears so I can hear my bros." Like many students across American campuses, Zack has been winking-in people who share his interests. "It's a good way to meet people," he says. "Like, let's say I want to meet a girl that likes to mush—bam—as long as she put that in her profile, I see her." While critics claim winking is an antisocial act, isolating users into a narrow range of preferences, many students believe it helps them save time and emotional space, allowing them to wink people out of their vision who otherwise would've taken weeks to reveal their incompatibility. Traci Hall says it has helped her eliminate unwanted ogling. "A lot of guys check me out and, before Winker, I'd have to walk to class and see every guy looking at me. Now I just wink in the type of guy I want, and all the others become blur-bodies."

2028 Nov 23 Joseph Yoon, *Atlanta Constitution* 1M (Lexis-Nexis): Intended for sex offenders, Winker's use of red-lining anyone with a criminal record raises a number of ethical issues. Take the case of Joshua Martin: his misdemeanor for ripping Inner-Ear downloads earned him four years as a red-body. "Anyone who's winking sees my red-body and crosses the street," Martin reports. He claims he lives in virtual isolation thanks to Winker.

WMDMA *n.* [after WMD (Weapons of Mass Destruction) + MDMA (see Ecstasy)]: Methamphetamines shaped like or named after weapons of mass destruction.

2028 Nov 1 Jonathan Wolfe, *The Oregonian* [Portland, OR]: This week's police raid on a Burnside Avenue apartment turned up a collection of KLMT-8 bomb-shaped ecstasy pills. In addition there were over one hundred Baggies of meth labeled White Phosphorous. "There's only so much you can do," said Sergeant Newman. "We can destroy this stuff, but there are plenty of other labs out there and a growing demand from elementary school kids on up." The drugs, known as WMDMA, have become common among Virtual Reality Raves, resulting in the recent deaths of Seattle partygoers who were online raving alone in their homes. Despite the rising toll of WMDMA-related deaths, Bausch & Cartz Pharmaceuticals believes the increase of amphetamine-based drugs reveals a vital need for stronger FDA-approved ADHD medication for preteens and young adults.

MOKSHA

I.

RUMOR WAS YOU could still find enlightenment in Nepal, and
for cheap. There were back rooms down the spiderwebbed
streets of Kathmandu where they wired you in, kicked on
the generator, and sent data flowing through your brain for
fifteen thousand rupees a session. It was true, Jeff from the
co-op had assured Abe, though passport control could be a
bitch when you returned to the States.

"They pulled my buddy when we hit Newark," Jeff had
said, sipping maté from a gourd. "But he was showing. His
third eye was completely open and he wanted to hug everyone. Just think about porn and you'll be fine." Jeff had handed
Abe a crinkled business card. *Namaste Imports.* "Go to this
place."

So Abe had saved his money, bought the ticket, and trav-
eled the endless hours, numbed by bad sleep and bland airline

food, to find himself in Kathmandu. Finding Namaste Imports, however, had proved impossible. The streets had no names and, looking up, all Abe saw was a tangle of electrical wires and lights blinking on in the dusk. Around him, masses of tourists, heavy with backpacks and vacant looks, milled about. And amid all this churned a perpetual stream of cars and mopeds, nudging their way around pedestrians, honking, yelling out of windows, and raising endless dust. It all seemed far from enlightenment.

By ten that night, the shops had shut down. Abe wandered back to his hotel to the sound of Beatles cover bands filtering down from terrace cafés. A couple skinny Nepali teens emerged from the darkness. "Hash, Pollen, Sex?" they asked, but when Abe asked for Moksha, they turned squirrelly and retreated back into the doorways. So Abe returned to his hotel room, stretched out on his bed, and wondered if it was all bullshit, and Jeff had sent him on a fool's errand that'd cost him his savings.

Moksha, it turned out, wasn't bullshit. It'd just gone into hiding ever since the twenties when the U.S. cracked down on Nepali distribution. There had been nonstop busts at yoga studios and health spas in the U.S. An oxygen bar in Sedona had been found with makeshift crown plates hooked up to an old Sega Genesis console. The CIA had confiscated the equipment and sentenced the owners, a gray-haired, dreadlocked couple, to life. By the time Abe was in high school, and just starting to get interested in experimenting with enlightenment, it was impossible to find. The U.S. government had strong-armed Eastern religions. Transcendental meditation classes were raided, tai chi groups disappeared from the parks, and churches began burning esoteric Buddhist texts. The closest Abe had come to scoring any enlightenment was when some seniors, troubled kids with a penchant for Lao-Tzu, had cannibalized an old iMac and built a crown plate out of tinfoil. Abe had placed the foil cap on his head and closed his eyes.

For a moment, sitting in the kid's garage on a nylon beach chair, Abe had thought he felt something. He sensed a dull light behind his eyes, fuzzy and warm, and his heartbeat expanded. The sound of the air-conditioning unit kicking on droned into a melody, and he'd had a vision of his mother asking him, as though he were still a child, if he wanted her to pack him a lunch. Light streamed through the window over the kitchen sink, and for a split second he saw her sadness. Then something in the makeshift machine popped, sending a curl of plastic smoke into the air. The seniors had yelled *shit* and poured their Pepsi on the electrical fire, and Abe found himself back in the dank, oil-stained garage, as unenlightened as he'd ever been.

Later that night, in the safety of his room, Abe thought of how stupid he'd been. The DEA had scanners to pick up the bioenergetic emissions of neighborhoods. He'd risked his freedom for a split-second vision of his mother in the kitchen. And so he'd shaken his head, looked at his psychedelic black-light poster of the Dalai Lama, and told himself he was a fucking idiot.

And yet, here he was in Nepal, having gambled everything on this trip, approaching yet another tourist shop to ask for Moksha. The store was crouched down a narrow side street behind Durbar Square, far from the streets of Thamel, where shops sold colorful yak scarves and were filled with desperate tourists looking for cheap prayer flags. There the shopkeepers all shook their heads when Abe asked for Moksha, telling him to buy a thangka painting instead. But here, amid the collapsing buildings, where the kids played on piles of rubble and bricks, was a small storefront. An old woman sat on a stool, barely visible amid the stitched bags and prayer bowls.

"Namaste," Abe said, and she answered by putting her palms together. "Moksha?" he asked.

She looked at him, her eyes silver between the lids. For a long time she said nothing, and Abe was about to give up when she asked, "How long you stay in Nepal?"

"Three weeks." That was as long as he'd given himself to find enlightenment.

"Why you look for Moksha?"

It was the first time he'd been asked directly, and Abe realized he had no real answer. She looked like she was about to shoo him away, so he settled on, "You can't get it in America."

She looked at him again and then closed her eyes. "Twenty-five thousand."

Jeff from the co-op had prepared him for the haggling, which wasn't simply expected but a kind of courtesy here. "Fifteen."

The old woman shook her head. "For fifteen you get peaceful insight instead."

"No, no, I want Moksha," Abe said. "Seventeen."

"Seventeen no good. Moksha use too much electricity, very expensive."

"Yeah, but my friend bought Moksha for fifteen thousand."

"This store?"

"Well, no, but—"

"Not same quality. Your friend only find lower stages of enlightenment. Here we have total enlightenment, better quality."

"No, my friend said he was totally enlightened," Abe said, though he had to admit, for all his talk about kundalini, Jeff from the co-op hadn't really seemed that enlightened.

"For you: twenty-three thousand. Best price. We go lower and I lose Moksha. Come." She rose from the stool and led Abe through the back of the store, which opened to a courtyard, and then into another building and up a dark, wet stairwell to knock at a closed door on the second floor.

Behind the door were the sounds of shuffling and the

distant chirp of dial-up connection. Then the door opened and a spiky-haired kid, no older than sixteen, stood in the doorway in a stained Bob Marley T-shirt. "You wait," he said, and closed the door. There was more shuffling; then the door opened again, and a white kid, his blue eyes shining, emerged with the light of rapture. Upon seeing Abe, he wrapped his arms around him for a long moment before whispering into Abe's ear, "Yes, brother, yes," and disappearing down the stairwell.

"You, Moksha, next," the spiky-haired kid said.

※

LONG BEFORE HE bought his ticket to Nepal and dropped out of the dumpy state college, he'd met Sandra. They'd seen each other in the basement of a record shop, at an underground dharma class run by some renegade Anthropology students. Abe and Sandra drank sake and talked about Zen Buddhism until the shop was raided and the university expelled the leaders for practicing walking meditation on campus. Later that winter, she'd told him how much Moksha scared her. Her father had become addicted when she was in middle school.

"He stopped talking for days at a time," she confided from beneath the sheets in Abe's dorm room. "He'd just sit on his cushion, wired up to our old Xbox, whispering *om mani padme hum.*"

Abe took a deep breath, held it, and let it out slowly. "So, you don't want to go to Nepal and become liberated?"

"My dad wasn't liberated; he thought finding enlightenment was more important than his family."

"Maybe he'd transcended attachment."

Sandra got up and dressed. "Whatever. Go to Nepal; become a self-centered asshole like my dad. I love you, but obviously that's not enough."

Abe had watched her, concentrating on his pounding heart to keep from speaking. After she left, he consoled himself with the *Tibetan Book of the Dead.* Sandra was just a hungry ghost, he told himself, offering the kind of love that kept people bound to the cycle of rebirth. All the same, he couldn't shake the fact that he'd probably never again wake with her in the small concrete-walled dorm of that unenlightened college town. That, and he wished they'd had sex before he'd talked about liberation.

✳

"OKAY," THE SPIKY-HAIRED boy said, "You sit there." He pointed to a corner in the darkened room.

The room was filled with gutted laptops, stray mice, and a cluster of computer towers interconnected by cables. There was a beauty salon chair next to the towers, an old model from the seventies, and the cables had been fitted into the blow-dryer crown. In the other corner of the room, near the blackened windows, two old men sat on the floor eating chal bhat and smoking cigarettes.

"Okay, Moksha," the kid said. "Get in."

Abe hesitated. Until now, he'd imagined he'd never find enlightenment. Faced with the beauty salon chair, he wasn't sure he was ready. What if, like Sandra's father, he became one of those modern-day sadhus who ate only raw food and talked about kombucha? He asked if he needed to do anything to prepare. Meditate? Breathe properly?

"No, just sit. We take care of Moksha."

Abe nodded and lowered himself into the chair. The kid dropped the blow-dryer cap onto Abe's head, logged on to the laptop by the side of the chair, and hit Enter.

The jolt of Moksha was immediate. One moment Abe was sitting in the chair, watching the men eat chicken curry, and wondering what enlightenment would feel like, and the next second their bodies transformed into bands of light. Where Abe had seen a dark cluttered space, it became apparent that the configuration of computer boxes, the pile of plastic water bottles, and the mess of disemboweled laptops formed a sacred geometry whose mandala spread outward past the walls. Abe could see through the bricks to perceive the entire city. Every shop shone brightly with its display of a hundred bronze Buddhas, and the taxis that cut their way through the crowds sent a chorus of honks into the air like birdsong. He saw the kids playing in the bricks, the white kid who had hugged him standing on the corner haggling for a yak blanket, the words leaving the kid's mouth as illuminated air currents. He saw the light of their hearts beating beneath their skin while above, and around, and inside them was a force so bright that to look at it directly was blinding. He told himself to look away, but it was too late; his limited ego that tried to hang on was of minuscule value in comparison to the illumination of the infinite. Abe turned his inner eyes to the blazing light, and in that moment there was nothing left: no Abe, no Kathmandu, no Buddha; all names burned in the fire, leaving only a vibration that could best be described as love.

Abe was certain he had died, but then he heard the kid's voice from far off. "Okay, all done." He felt the dryer lift from his head and found himself back in the room.

"Oh my God," he uttered and grasped the boy's arm.

"Yeah, okay, goodbye now. Next customer waiting."

Abe was lifted to his feet and he stood wobbly, feeling a great urge to hug the young boy, who was already leading him to the door. On the other side stood a frazzle-haired girl in yoga pants wearing dozens of beaded necklaces. Abe saw the Western pain in her eyes, and his heart blossomed. He threw his arms around her.

"It's okay," he whispered. "You've already got it. We've all got it." He would have hung on, but he felt her fear, so he released her and made his way down the dark, wet staircase with his palms open to the world and the glorious sunlight of Kathmandu.

II.

ENLIGHTENMENT, IT TURNED out, didn't last long.

By the next morning, Abe could already feel the hooks of samsara tethering him to the bed. He worried about his return to the States and his menial job brewing lattes at the co-op. He found himself irritated by the noise of Kathmandu, the dust, his dirty clothes, which stank of sweat, and the humidity that already drenched his body. And so he dressed and returned to the small shop to pay his twenty-three thousand rupees. He tasted Moksha again, only to come crashing down later that evening, realizing with deep terror that, at this rate, he wouldn't have enough money to last him until the end of the month.

That evening he ended up drinking at a rooftop bar, where he poured his heart out to a Dutch tourist with enlightened eyes and a Ganesha tank top. "You can't find *real* enlightenment in the city," the Dutchman said. "You need to go to the Muktinath temple in the mountains."

"And they have M at the temple?"

"No, it's just an old temple. But find the Muktinath Guesthouse. Amazing M, much cheaper than here. Good masala tea, too," the Dutchman promised. And Abe, who had begun to sense a kind of spiritual emptiness, felt hopeful again.

To get to the fabled city of Muktinath proved difficult. It required a ten-hour bus ride, followed by an early morning flight into the Annapurna mountains. From there it was another three-hour jeep ride and finally a half-mile walk through the dusty mountain village to the Muktinath Guesthouse—a damp, rotting wood hostel filled with stoned backpackers carrying ukuleles.

Up here, far from the watchful eye of the CIA and Kathmandu police, things were more lax. The Moksha Room was full of computer stations, where old and young alike reclined day and night, getting data shot through their crown chakras for five thousand rupees a pop. The guesthouse had upgraded its equipment, allowing users to add music to their enlightenment sessions. Abe could choose from acid jazz, Afrobeat, and dub reggae, the music crescendoing as his ego was peeled away, and he would emerge onto the upstairs balcony, beneath the starry sky, to find fellow Moksha-fueled backpackers giving impromptu lectures on the Bardo realms of reincarnation and the benefits of coconut water.

The guesthouse proved to be the kind of communal ashram that Abe had always imagined. He, who had read a contraband, alligator-clipped, *Egyptian Book of the Dead* beneath bedcovers in high school, was now lounging with international backpackers and smoking hashish on the outside deck; drawing diagrams of the chi meridian system in the back of Lonely Planet guidebooks; and singing devotional songs to Shiva.

It was true, Abe admitted to a beautiful young woman

from Santa Cruz, Moksha was the best. "Have you heard of Satori?" she asked. Abe hadn't. "You can only get it in Tokyo. You use goggles and totally perceive nothingness. Kind of like Moksha but black-hole style, if you know what I mean."

"Cool," Abe said, though he wondered if he fully understood. While most of the guests at the lodge spoke about nothingness, Abe increasingly found himself returning to a deep something he couldn't shake. Perhaps it was the spotty connection.

"Moksha's fun but kinda boring. I mean, compared to Sufi Trance, there's no comparison. I would do Trance any night. You just spin and spin and spin," she said.

"Wow."

"Yeah, it's super sexy." She took a drag of her cigarette, the wetness of her lips catching the moonlight.

"You know, I really like you," Abe said.

She kept her gaze focused on the moon. "That's sweet," she said, "but I only go for saints and sadhus. It's nothing personal. You've just still got a long path to walk."

Abe wished she'd say more, but she didn't. They were in the post-Moksha space, where words were superfluous and creation reverberated in his ears with the echoes of dial-up. So Abe consoled himself with the knowledge that they didn't need to have sex to be eternally connected as sacred partners, and this turned out for the best, as she left the next morning to catch a plane to Goa, where she'd heard there were really amazing Trance raves.

III.

ON THE DAY of his departure, Abe had precisely enough to pay for his lodging, the travel back to Kathmandu, and finally a taxi to the airport. It was clear: there'd be no more Moksha. He folded his dirty laundry into his backpack and bowed namaste to the bedroom with its itchy sheets and spotty electricity, then went to pay his bill.

Besides the clerk at the desk, the guesthouse was silent, and Abe emerged onto the dusty street without a farewell. Looking up the road, he could see the temple high above. It was said there were 108 spouts at the highest peak of the temple, which poured mountain water upon the heads of willing pilgrims. You could undress and pass beneath the rushing water, full of the scent of earth, and in doing so finally experience true liberation. He'd never made the trek to see it. No one at the guesthouse had, it seemed; they stayed on the porch smoking joints or sung by the fireplace. Garuda, a self-proclaimed Mahavishnu from New Jersey, had scoffed at the idea. "All you do up there is turn prayer wheels and light incense," he'd said, and Abe had felt incredibly foolish for asking. But here, in the morning light, Indian tourists in their *dhotis* walked by, bringing with them aunts, uncles, grandparents, and children. They looked sincere and hopeful with a levity Abe couldn't place. They were families, human in their unenlightenment, but happy. Abe watched the pilgrims passing, and then he joined the group, heading past the street vendors toward the temple above.

The day was already warm and, with the weight of the backpack, Abe was sweating by the time he reached the zigzagging path that led to the temple gates. Ash-covered sadhus sat by the entrance with their chillums and begging bowls, surrounded by white mountain rocks and wind. On the other side, the world was green. A great river ran through the temple, and from its banks bamboo rose tall. Prayer bells hung along the path, and far ahead were the large bathing pools. Men and women were in various stages of undress, some entering the soaking pool, others climbing the final steps to the spouts carved with the faces of Gods. Abe took off his shoes and socks, and stripped off his pants, and stood in line in his boxers amid the burning incense.

Soon he'd be back on a plane, surrounded by pressurized air and bland airline food. His parents would be upset with him when he returned home; they'd lecture him about dropping out of college and wasting his money. But they'd be happy to see him, and he could tell them about liberation. The line moved forward. Mostly, he'd just be happy for a soft bed. He thought of the guesthouse's bedroom—how it had smelled of fryer oil and the sweat of previous guests—and then about his old dorm room, where Sandra and he had spent their nights. He would call her when he got home. It was likely she wouldn't want to talk. If she did, she'd remind him how all he'd ever spoken about was Moksha. But if she let him, he'd tell her about the vision he'd had so many times after his enlightenment sessions. A memory of a late afternoon when they'd walked across campus to her dorm room to make love. They'd leaned against one another as they walked, and he'd noticed the sound of the leaves around their feet, and the air that was cold with winter, and he'd felt her love surrounding him. Abe would tell her about how he'd be happy just to be back on campus together with her, taking a walk. The line moved forward again. Who knew, maybe these fountains would liberate him from such desires, but maybe he'd simply be happy to be beneath the blankets in her dorm room, watching a movie and eating popcorn as they'd done back in the days when he was unenlightened. It was his turn. Abe closed his eyes and bowed his head and stepped forward.

The water, it turned out, was freezing.

CHILDREN OF THE
NEW WORLD

SOMETIMES, WHEN EVENING comes and the light hits our home in a way that reminds us of that other life, we'll talk about them. What their faces looked like, the feeling of their weight in our arms, the way our youngest would crawl onto my back. I'll see Mary sitting alone in our living room, the sun gone, just the reds of dusk outlining the trees, and I know she's remembering them. I walk over, put my arms around her, or kneel by her and place my head in her lap, and we'll stay like that, holding one another's pain, wondering whether we are truly monsters.

They weren't real, we say, looking for confirmation. Right?

Right.

Then we get up, start dinner, and move on with our child-less lives.

✸

FOR THOSE OF us who became parents in those first years, we remember the awe and beauty of the New World. To lie down in the darkness of the compartment, adjust the pillow beneath our heads, and log on was tantalizing. The chamber's darkness gave way to the light of the other world, the white walls of our online home appearing before us, filling our teeth with electric joy. We recall the first steps we took in our new house. To reach out and touch the world was to be illuminated, and we walked outside to see the homes lined up along our street shining and new, other users emerging from doorways, waving as they crossed their lawns to make introductions. Isn't this incredible? Where are you using from? Las Cruces, Copenhagen, Austin. We were like babies. Like Adam and Eve, some said. We reached out toward each other to see how skin felt; we let our neighbors' hands run across our arms. In this world, we seemed to understand, we were free to experience a physical connection that we'd always longed for in the real world but had never been able to achieve. Who can blame us for being reckless?

Perhaps such thoughts seem childish now, in light of all that happened; yet it's often those first weeks of usage, when the world was still new, that Mary and I speak of most when we remind ourselves that life was good. It was just a beautiful illusion, we tell each other, a fantastic electronic diversion. Right? Right, we say.

MARY'S PREGNANCY TOOK us both by surprise. She had gone through menopause a decade earlier and we'd resigned ourselves to living childless lives. We'd waited too long, had debated the pros and cons too many times, had placed our jobs first, and then it was too late. It was only when Mary's belly began to swell that we accessed the FAQ tab. It was all there, no great mystery: pregnancy worked the same as in the real world, fully explained in the tutorial. We had planned to watch the walk-thru at some point, had gotten as far as the instruction to roll our thoughts to the left to select our tattoos and piercings, up and down for musculature and age, but then we began playing with landscapes and play-lists, and before we knew it, we had the basics of navigation down. This is how you upload music to the home speakers; this is how you project your photos onto the living room wall; this is how you place one hand on your wife's hips; this is how she puts her hand behind your neck; this is how you kiss. And then she was pregnant.

The FAQs informed us we could remove an unwanted pregnancy as easily as dragging a file to the recycle bin, but we were curious. Here would be another being formed from the combination of our genome preferences. The birth promised to be as quick and painless as a download. So we held each other, scrolled through online baby names, and agreed to bring new life into this world.

In the New World, Mary and I proved to be a completely different couple. Our bodies became freed from habit, independent of hormonal changes. We grew hungry for the electric hum of each other. Mary soon became pregnant again and our lives were illuminated in a way we'd thought impossible in the physical world. Online, with our new family, we had found joy.

※

JUNE HAD JUST turned three, Oscar two, when Mary and I began to explore the borders of the New World. By then most everyone had heard of the Dark City. It was there on the horizon, out over the tree line of our neighborhood, a brown glow in the distance. It was common knowledge you could travel to the city to spend a few hours, days even, among its pleasure domes and massage parlors. When I'd log off and go to work, the other men at the office made jokes about their weekends, a delicious guilt within their laughter. Smoothest bodies you'll ever feel, they confided. It was said there were parlors where air currents tickled the body to the edge of orgasm. There were morphing temples where skin became ecstatic mounds of quivering jelly. We were intrigued. I'd go if you went, we agreed. So, one night late in January, after the children had fallen asleep, we left them with an online babysitter and headed for the Dark City.

I'd once witnessed Amsterdam's Red Light district with its windows of naked bodies and its rotten maroon lights. I can still smell its cobblestones, thick with dirt, and see the doorways, dark with hungry faces. This was what I'd imagined the Dark City would resemble, and I'd expected to be repulsed when we approached its gates, to turn back with shame and relief, to write the place off as a tasteless distraction. But, though the city oozed a seedy brown light, up close the streets were lit by warm yellow lamps, humming with electricity. The gates of its many entrances stood open, so welcoming that turning away was impossible. We saw men and women emerging from its depths, setting off from the gates to return home. There was no danger in exploring a block or two, we reasoned.

So we entered the first district of the city, filled with its soft-core delights, its toy shops and kissing booths. The stores reflected the amber glow of lamps, which brightened the faces of other tourists who walked the streets: couples with their arms around each other, college kids sitting on curbs kissing, single men walking with their hands in their pockets. A Korean man standing by a foot massage parlor called out to us, "Beautiful Asian girls. Twenty credits for fifteen minutes." Across the street, a gorgeous man called my wife sweetie and invited us inside to be tickled. And rising above the lights and the busy streets, one could hear the collective moans from deep within the web of avenues, pulling us forward toward the core, where we longed to play.

The Air Current Hotels were four blocks in. White three-story buildings with darkened windows and velvet ropes leading to their doors. At the check-in desk, a teenage receptionist in a string-top charged my account forty credits for the session.

"It's our first time."

"You'll love it!" she said. "You've never experienced air like this!" She smiled and directed us toward the elevators. "Second floor, room number seventeen."

"What do we do there?"

"Just close the door and stand in the middle of the room. We'll take it from there."

We rode the elevator to the second floor and found the room entirely empty, the lights dimmed. I shut the door behind us, and we stepped into the middle of the room. A light draft played along the floor, working its way up my pant legs and finding the softness behind my knees. Another breeze caressed my neck, then slid down my collar. Our feet were lifted from the ground and we floated horizontally, air currents tickling our skin with alternating nips of cold and warmth. Wind rubbed against my lips, playing against my tongue; a strong gust pushed against my chest, holding me down. I reached out to hold on to Mary, but there was nothing except air, and I was filled with the luxurious thought that I was being made love to by a goddess of wind. Mary arched her back, pushing down into the gusts that caressed her again and again, until her body was vibrating, piqued by wind, and we blossomed together, our bodies becoming one with the network of electrons buzzing around us.

In this way, Mary and I became one of the many couples walking with their arms around each other, post-orgasmic and giddy, on the streets of the Dark City. We graduated from the Air Current Hotels to the Thousand-Finger Parlors—where we lay with our eyes closed, holding each other's hands as invisible fingers rubbed us to climax—and later on to the second ring of the city, with its Morphing Temples. We explored our bodies as sea creatures and woodland animals. Mary would transform into a blue-eyed doe, and I, a buck, would brush my antlers against her fur as I mounted her. There was a beautiful playfulness to it all, and we rekindled our passion, which was restricted to our online lives. For when we returned to our chambers at home and changed out of our clothes, we did so with cybernetic exhaustion, barely noticing our naked bodies, which brushed against each other in the bathroom. And when we kissed goodnight, we didn't linger. This, however, seemed a small price to pay for our online pleasures, and if we felt disconnected from each other in the real world, we attempted to pay this little heed, focusing instead on that moment, every night, when our children were asleep and we'd set off to seek our individual pleasures together.

※

MARY FOUND THE man in our bathroom shortly after we'd visited the Bondage Cathedral. I heard her scream from the other side of the house. He stood there, his body flickering—a low-resolution, pale-faced man whose body pixelated in places. His erection, however, glowed in high resolution, and when he saw Mary he said, "I want to please you in sixty-nine ways," before she slammed the door shut and yelled for help. When I opened the door, the man was stroking himself, looking down at his enormous penis. "I can help you grow three inches naturally," he told me.

The FAQs didn't cover this. And it was only after searching through other users' blog entries that we figured out how to delete him from our home. But during our next session, when the doorbell rang, we opened the front door and encountered a man from Ghana who told us he was a distant relative. He'd brought our children presents, he said. He needed our credit number to upload the toys for the kids. We locked the door but we could see the man outside, pacing first on our porch, and then climbing into our bushes to knock on our windows. We deleted the African man, but when night came, our lamps no longer lit our home with soft warmth but contained a shadowy light, and our house was filled with the feeling of being watched by countless eyes, our every action scanned for information.

Mary took the children into our bedroom, and I logged off to call online support. The man on the other end of the line spoke broken English, the line buzzing from an overseas connection. He tried a couple options with me, and finally said, "Sir, your account is corrupted. You will have to reset all files to the initial settings."

"What's that mean?"

"You must delete all data from your account—your preferences, photos, and music. You will need to re-create your bodies again. I see you have children."

"Yes."

"You will need to delete them."

"What?"

"The virus has spread to them. You will have to delete them and begin again. I'm sorry, sir."

"I'm not deleting my children!"

"Yes, sir, I understand. It is your choice. But the system has a fatal error; it will only get worse. Your account is filled with viruses. You will not want your children in that house soon."

"Put your supervisor on."

"Yes, sir," the man said. Then I was put on hold for ten minutes of light jazz until a supervisor, and later her supervisor, told me the same information: that we should have installed an anti-virus protection plan. Without it, there was little left to do but return our system to factory settings.

"What if we move to a new house?"

"I'm afraid all of your family is corrupted," the supervisor told me. "You'll just end up bringing the virus with you. It's an easy process to reboot. Simply hold down the power button on your console for twenty seconds and—"

"These are my children!" I yelled.

"If it's any consolation, they won't feel a thing; they're just data."

I hung up the phone and told Mary the news. There was no way, we agreed, that we would reboot. We'd have to be vigilant, delete each and every file when they appeared. The kids could sleep in our room; we'd take shifts keeping watch over them. I called in sick to work and Mary used her vacation days, but within a week nowhere was safe. A bronze-skinned man with spiky hair appeared in our bedroom, telling Mary there were guys like him waiting to connect with her. A woman who looked like my mother transmogrified in the living room, saying she'd been robbed and needed our help to pay for groceries. We had to restrain our children from running to her when she called out their names. Toys began appearing around the house; to touch a single one was to transmit all our information across an unsecure interface. We hid the children beneath blankets, telling them this was all a game we were playing. And then, one evening, we found ourselves surrounded, every room of the house filled with cartoon characters hawking downloadable games and attractive women selling vibrators and wrinkle cream.

"We don't have a choice," I finally said to Mary. "You can stay with them and hold them. I'll log out and do it."

"Do what, Daddy?" June asked, peeking out from the hut we'd built in the corner of our bedroom. We were silent for a moment.

"Nothing," I said quietly. "Come and give me a hug. You, too, Oscar," I called, and our children emerged from the hut, climbing onto my lap to put their arms around me.

I often tell myself that I held them for as long as I could. It was worse for Mary; she felt their bodies disappear from beneath her embrace.

※

AMONG MY FAVORITE memories: Snow. Its enhanced crystalline structure; its pristine whiteness; its silence. Oscar, June, and I on a sled, zooming down a snowy hill, which spools endlessly ahead of us, June pointing at the corn-piped snowman bowing to us and tipping his top hat as we speed by. And when we walk back to the house, our sled dragging behind us, the quiet end of the day, dusk falling along the horizon, the snow lilac with evening.

Mary's favorite memory: A morning in spring, the soft light breaking through our windows and lighting up the wood floors. I'm playing with June, rolling a small Matchbox car back and forth, and Oscar is sleeping in her arms, our family together and quiet in the morning light.

Things I regret: raising my voice. The look of surprise on their faces moments before the hurt set in. And for what? For taking too long putting on their shoes; for not wanting to sleep when I was ready to log off; for asking me to read another chapter; for being children. There's no way you can give everything to your children, no way you can spend every minute with them or be there for each hour of their lives. But give me a second chance, and I'd never log off. I'd read them stories until they were deep asleep, hold them tightly through the darkness, and tell them I loved them once again. The feeling of parenthood never leaves you. Not when I go to work now. Not when Mary and I go to dinner or sit alone at the movie theater.

✺

EVERY SUNDAY, MARY and I go to the support group they hold over in Corvallis at the community center. It's facilitated by Bill Thompson, a large, heavyset man with a salt-and-pepper beard who reminds us of a grizzly bear. He's a warm-hearted guy, gruff in a comforting way, who smokes Marlboro Reds outside during breaks. Every meeting he brings a basket of assorted teas and coffee for us, arranges our chairs in a circle, and offers a hug more readily than a handshake. One of his common pieces of wisdom is, "Don't let anyone tell you they weren't real." He puts his fingers over his heart and taps softly. "They were real here." Of everyone who attends, he's undoubtedly lost the most; he had a family of five and a wife he'd met online who turned out to be a scammer. She'd taken it all from him: drained his savings, stolen his identity, and infected the children. Not that we should compare losses, he tells us. There's no hierarchy to pain. "Our work isn't to figure out who hurts the most," he says. "Our work is to heal."

We take turns. New members tell their stories first. They go through the stages many of us have gone through. They show us their photos—if they're lucky enough to have printed them—they talk about the smell of their children, the colors of the clothing they were wearing on the last day before they rebooted. They cry, and Bill holds the space for them, gives them a hug when it seems like they'll accept one, and teaches us how to grieve. "We all have to reboot *this*," he says, and motions to the room with his open palms. "This world, with all its pain and loss. This is where we learn to love again."

Bill's been a real savior to Mary and me. For a long time there was no one to share our pain with. We have friends and they're good-hearted, well-meaning people, but they never had kids on the other side. They comfort us for a while, a couple weeks, a month; they send sympathy cards and flowers, but in the end they all offer the same advice: It's time to move on. They were just programs. You can create new children. And we nod grimly, knowing full well we'll never return.

Bill's advice has helped us get to a place where we can say what happened wasn't our fault, that we're not monsters, that our children didn't die because of us. We were lonely. We were needful. We wanted to feel pleasure again, to be caressed and loved. Our longings were those of humans, not monsters. No, the real monsters in this world are the hackers and scammers, faceless men and women who destroy lives for the joy of testing a virus, and who sacrificed our children to make a buck.

When the meetings are over, Bill invites us to be physical like we were in the other world. "Human contact is all there really is," he says. And so we put our arms around one another, timidly at first, and eventually, with all the warmth of our bodies. We hold the others who come, the parents and widowers, the aunts, uncles, and grandparents. We pull strangers into our embrace and hold them tightly against us. There's nothing electronic about the gesture, no hum to the body, only the warmth of their breathing and the beating of their hearts.

FALL LINE

I'M FILLING ICE when Sunny radios that Desolation Pass is officially closed for the season. The top half is skiable, but after that it's all patches of grass and rocks. "I'll tell them to bring an inner tube," I radio back, and Sunny says in his Cali drawl, "Riiiiight." Ever since the Big Thaw, anyone wanting diamonds needs to buy a ticket to Dubai and shred indoor slopes. For the past three years, all we've had is slush and mud patches that catch your edge and leave you soaked and miserable by the end of the day. Even the hard-core skiers don't bother going out more than once or twice a season. There will be flurries, the temp drops to thirty, and you get that phantom itch to grind bumps. Then you take the first run, mash through freezing crud, skid on a patch of ice, and realize why you don't ski anymore.

The lodge is quiet, chairs still on the tables, just a group of old-timers changing into their boots—diehards who've been coming since the turn of the millennium, back when you could still catch knee-deep powder and the bar was standing-room only after the lifts closed. They're all in their seventies and I wonder why they bother. The slopes are hell on the knees, but still they boot up and hit the runs for their weeklong vacation.

"Think we're going to see some powder?" one of them asks.

"Sure, right over there," I say and motion to the flat-screen, where we're playing old X-Sports clips. Bonnie Hale is doing a 360 off a Kilimanjaro peak.

"Have faith," another one of the guys says, and they lower their goggles and go trudging out.

That leaves the only other two in the room, a little girl sitting on the bench and her dad struggling to get her suited up. Our kiddie hills are dotted with toddlers and their parents who want them to experience skiing before it's gone. Sunny runs a ski school, which manages to barely be worth his time. He's got half a dozen kids booked in his morning class, another five in his afternoon Little Eskimo Club.

My agent found me this gig when I got out of recovery. It was becoming clear to him that I wasn't ever going to return to the circuit, stomp powder again, make real money. He said a lodge in Utah wanted me to teach classes.

"No fucking way I'm doing bunny slopes."

"All right, then let me ask you a question: When's the comeback?"

"Soon," I said.

"Uh-huh. You've been saying that for four years."

"I was learning to walk for the first three of them."

"Ronnie, you need to take this job. I can't line up any more interviews if you don't ski. People are forgetting about you."

I didn't take the job, and that summer my agent dumped me. I coasted on savings and posted updates on my Third Eye feed—mostly me lifting weights, going to physical therapy— but my followers were dwindling. I watched my feed drop below a million. Then I started bartending at Red Lobster, serving old biddies who had no clue who I was, and it depressed me enough to call the lodge and agree to work a season.

Rick, the mountain manager, wanted me to give extreme lessons. He figured he'd cash in while I was still alive in people's memory. *Extreme ski with Ronnie Hawks: Big Snow Gold Medalist and Xtreme Games Champion.* I agreed, and though Third Eye's focus fades as quickly as the next viral video, it worked. Old fans logged on to my feed and actually came to the mountain to learn tricks from me.

It wasn't an extreme class. No cliffs, no 540 tail grabs or Lincoln loops, nothing that could break a neck or put some-one in the hospital. What we had was a groomed slope with a couple packed jumps where I taught aging millennials how to do a daffy, a spread eagle, a backscratcher for the most advanced. We had a rail and a half-pipe, and I demonstrated combo grinds, watching as one after the other busted their asses. Every now and then I'd get a kid who wanted me to teach him a switched cork or backflip, and I'd put my glove beneath my chin, out of camera range, and point at my eyes. "Sorry, man, not allowed," I'd say, which was my way of letting him know that if it wasn't for the contacts, I'd have done it. The lodge made us keep them in so skiers could beam into any lift operator's eyes and see the unbroken lines of snow or follow ski patrol to find out where the powder runs were. That's a joke now—our streams are basically a bad version of the nature channel. You can watch empty ski lift after empty ski lift if that's what gets you off, maybe see a single coyote make its way through the mush.

I made good tips and usually got free drinks. Everyone wanted to know about the accident, what it felt like to drop off that cliff, go tumbling halfway down a rock face, how I could ever bring myself to put on skis again. If they were fans, I'd drag the story out for as many rounds as I needed to get plastered.

"It hurt like hell," I'd tell whoever was buying. It sucked. But your bones healed and you got over it, because you don't give in to fear—not in life and not in extreme powder. "Give in to fear and you might as well give up on living," I'd say, just like I had in all the post-crash interviews. People wanted to hear that my crash was a metaphor for their lives: overcome the odds; don't give up no matter how hard you fall. It was symbolic to them, and they'd go back to their office jobs imagining they were applying my philosophy when they were turned down for a promotion. What they didn't want to hear was how my bones screamed at night so bad I had to smoke

enough weed to get a busload stoned to fall asleep; how maybe
I'd put on skis and do a rail slide, but there was no way I'd
ever go off a cliff again; how my career officially ended when
I fucked up that jump, and all that was left for me was a stupid extreme class, a couple last retrospectives, and free drinks
at Jerry's Lodge.

When people still remembered me, I could end a night
with a snowbunny. We'd take the shuttle down to Bear Ridge
and the girls would run their hands over my scars and see the
tattoos I'd gotten inked to cover the worst of my wounds.
"Feel this," I'd tell them, guiding their fingers along the
firebird that spreads its wings across my left hip. Sympathy
medicine, Jerry, the old bartender, used to call it. He said the
crash was the best thing that ever happened to me. "Man, if
I could go home with as many chicks as you, I'd ski off a cliff
any day."

"Yeah right," I'd say, thinking, *No you wouldn't.* Not if
you knew what it was like to spend three years in recovery
you wouldn't, not if you had to learn to walk again you
wouldn't, not if you knew how bones can scream, you sure
fucking wouldn't.

❋

THE WINTER AFTER I got out of recovery, X-Sports did a final
documentary on me, pitched as a comeback story. When I get
in a real dark place, I'll open a brew, vape some medical, and
watch it. The first half shows me stomping every mountain

known to man. It's sick. I achieved first descents on every continent; fucking dominated big mountain skiing. There's no doubt I was the best extreme skier out there. Then we hit *the fatal mistake*. Usually I'll fast-forward through that section—but nights when I'm real low I'll just sit there, the weight of Sour Diesel keeping me pinned. I see myself heading toward the cliff I never should've taken. I'd spotted the jutting ledges from the helicopter, marked it as a no-go, but the mountain stoked my ego and, in a split-moment decision, I wrecked my life thinking I could conquer anything. Fast-forward through my recovery, my parents saying they know I'll pull through, my buddies saying I'm the gnarliest skier alive and there's no way I'm ever going to stop rocking trails. And then there's me, learning to walk again, three years sped up to make it look like five minutes. The doctors predicted I'd never walk, but I fought against it, stopped taking the drugs, chewed through the pain to avoid the sleepy numbness, forced myself to try. The video doesn't show any of that, just hints at my return to skiing as I take my first steps out of the hospital.

The biography ends with me getting back on my skis and teaching my pathetic extreme class. "Nowadays, Ronnie's getting his confidence back and teaching a new crop of skiers how to tackle the mountains he once conquered." There's a clip of me doing a fakie off a rail and a small group of students clapping. "He's getting ready to take on his old nemesis, and when he does, you can bet we'll be there." They fade out on the Neacola range, the very mountain that ate me, and the implied promise that I'll rise to fight that cliff again. And that's it: a comeback story without a comeback. When I didn't return to extreme skiing, the interviews stopped. If I wasn't willing to risk my life, the media wasn't interested in following me. No blood, no money.

A year later the thaw began and I got a pass from Mother Nature. I escaped with the dignity of my promised return; it wasn't my fault I never went back, just the sorry state of the environment. But everybody knew the truth—my buddies, the videographer, big mountain skiers like Ethan Perdergast and Sean Godly—the sky could've dumped snow for the next hundred years, and I never would've gotten into another copter to pick my line toward that cliff.

※

ANGIE COMES IN at ten to help me get set up for the lunch rush—which is a joke; there's no rush, just the Little Eskimo Club wanting pizza and hot cocoa, followed by a few beginners and the ancient warriors who order wings, burgers, and fries. Angie takes drink orders while I work the grill.

"Hope you have a second keg ready for *the whiteout*," she says as we watch the scattered groups eating beneath the dimmed lights. Yesterday we had another bunk report of a storm coming our way.

"Counting on that blizzard," I say and wink.

"I'd be happy for six inches."

"There I can help you."

She leans her hip against the bar. "You wish," she says, and throws an ice cube at me, which lands on the flattop and sizzles.

We've been flirting ever since she started two years ago. What I liked about Angie was she wasn't a skier, just wanted to learn before it was all gone. When Rick introduced us, he said, "This here's the great Ronnie Hawks," and she just said *hey* and shook my hand, taking me for another ponytailed, tattooed washout—which I guess is close to the truth. Eventually, she found out about my history. You can't pass a season of dead days at the bar, watching old X-Sports videos on our flat-screen, without seeing me in the powder. But she didn't care much about that, only said to me one night, "Checked out your fall online, sorry about the wipeout." We worked bar together her first season, and though she's in her late thirties and I'm a decade younger, we hooked up that winter and passed a season together before our breakup.

"So, you figure out what you're going to do when summer comes?" I ask her and drop in an order of fries.

"Probably go to Brazil. Help rebuild after the floods."

"You're really going to do that?"

"Sure, why not? People need help, they need homes. They'll give me meals, a place to sleep—it's not like I'll earn anything, but hopefully I can do some good. You should think about volunteering."

I shrug my shoulders. "Thanks, but I'll probably just find a bartending gig in Ogden."

In January, Rick told us the news that the mountain was closing. After seventy-eight years, this would be our last season. He shut the lifts early one Monday—there was no one on the mountain—and we sat in the cafeteria while he dropped the bomb. Zeke, an old wiry guy with a frost-white beard, who's been here longer than all of us and boards like a monster, slammed his hat onto the table, got up, and left.

"Zeke, wait," Rick said, but Zeke was gone. Rick turned back to us. "Well, I'm devastated, too."

That was probably true. Our mountain had been a sleepy little place, run by locals, until it got discovered by a hedge fund exec who figured he'd make it the next Vail. He put in a bunch of lodges, some high-end boutiques, raised the ticket prices, and then the snow stopped. And here was Rick, who'd followed corporate's orders as best he could, had listened to a kid who wore a collared shirt instead of a ski jacket, and now he was about to be laid off like the rest of us. "It sucks," Rick admitted. "Totally *fucking* sucks, but what are we going to do? There's no snow anymore. Just try to enjoy the last season."

So that night, we all got sloshed, and Sunny and his band cranked up their guitars and rocked out till three in the morning, screaming into the microphone until they were hoarse, and it sounded like shit, but we didn't care. We danced, and

Angie and I made out behind the bar, and we tried to forget the blow of the bad news.

※

IN THE VIDEO clip that plays on repeat at the lodge, I'm standing atop Alaska's range, the helicopter lifting off-screen, and below me is untracked powder, line after perfect line, spines rising like a dragon's back. You look down through my eyes, and all you can see are cornices and big air about to get stomped. It's enough to make your heart stop. The copter's gone, wind chill's minus three, and I look down those spines, the holy grail of the Neacolas, and know I can mash it. Watch now as I set off, first turn a perfect carve, hit the lip and free-fall over two hundred feet, hurling carcass in a straight drop, land it flawless, sluff tumbling around me as I hit the next cliff. From the copter you see me nailing every turn along the razor-sharp spine, flying now, suspended above snow and mountain as I glide, then down again in an arc of snow, sunlight hitting me in late morning shine, everything perfect.

What I wanted was every mountain in the world geo-mapped into my brain and the ability to find a line through the sickest deathmakers. What I didn't want: a low-octane life of draining jobs, counting the days till I'd have time to mow the lawn again, counting the weeks till I could afford some plastic, beach-chair vacation, counting the years till retirement when I'd be too old to enjoy it. I was from a place built off those blueprints, where sprinklers went off in the morning and whole neighborhoods became ghost towns during work hours. I'd look out at all those empty houses, the exhausted adults returning home, the whole sorry bunch living at low throttle, and it seemed like death. I wanted to see the stars over Kilimanjaro, the sunrise after sleeping at the base of a killer range, to breathe powder. You can stand on the peak of the world, knowing you're about to drop into the mouth of a canyon sculpted by wind, and if you die, at least you die by your own rules. That's why I gave my life to extreme sports.

When I broke it all down to Angie like that, the winter we were together, poured my heart out as we finished a bottle of Jameson, she'd looked at me with something far from compassion.

"Fuck you," she finally said.

"What do you mean, 'fuck you'?"

"So, you skied like a maniac—you were great—whatever, you were fucking incredible. So what? What have you ever added to the world? You know those people you don't want to be like? All those people living their shitty, empty lives? Those are my parents you're talking about. That's me. That's my sister. That's most of the world. And maybe my parents aren't climbing ice faces with clamp-ons to go pick lines in wherever-the-fuck Alaska, but they worked hard to give me and my sister a good life, be there for us, to make a family."

"I'm not saying that isn't important—"

"Yes, you are. You fucking are. I mean, what's your life goal besides getting high and making out with me?"

Before my accident, my goal had been to ski until I died, or at least till my late thirties, then retire and spend my days signing merchandise contracts, and I'd never questioned staying viral on Third Eye. It was just something you did, a way to not be selfish. Kids in wheelchairs had tuned in to my contacts to see what it was like to mash the sweetest ranges in the world, and I shared the sunrises I witnessed rather than keeping them all for myself. Mostly I just wanted to find the courage to ski down a cliff face, catch it on Third Eye, have the video go viral and make me a celebrity again.

"I guess to shred a cliff again," I finally admitted.

"You know what my goal is?" she said. "To have kids, raise a family, take them on those vacations you hate so much. And I don't need to find the biggest wave, or the tallest peak, or whatever-the-fuck to feel alive. That's juvenile."

I knew I was drunk and I ought to be careful with my words, but when you were once the number-one freestyle skier in the world, it's easy to believe you owed it to others to focus on yourself. I'd shredded the most beautiful mountains, smoked killer weed, had sex with gorgeous women who thought I was a god. I'm not saying I wasn't a douche; I'm just saying that looking at my life, I couldn't figure out what was so wrong with it. "Well, I do need that," I said, "and all I'm doing is working at a fucking bar and stranded here with you."

"Nice," she said, and got up. "Actually, you're stranded here alone."

That was the end of us as a couple. We patched things up—what else can you do when you work bar shifts together five days a week—and we stayed friends, became ex-lovers who liked to flirt and hook up when we weren't together with anyone, but whatever future we'd had was gone. It was only after she'd broken up with me that I realized being with her was actually the only really good thing I'd had in years.

※

IT'S NOT A bad crowd for a Sunday night. Between the staff, the group of guys on their weeklong, and the day visitors, we're probably thirty strong and people are ordering baskets of wings, fries, onion rings, keeping me busy. I've got my back to the counter, dropping basket after basket of mozzarella sticks while Angie's punching in tabs, refilling pitchers, and leaning over the bar to get orders. Sunny and the Sunshine Band have set up in the corner and they're blasting the place with retro hits; a couple folks are even up dancing.

"Is this what the old days were like?" Angie asks and slides a pint of Powder Pale Ale next to me.

"Nah," I say and take a drink, looking out at the aging crowd. "It used to be wall-to-wall snowbunnies."

The band takes a break and Sunny comes over. "Temperature's dropping," he says, and Angie pours him a pint. "Check it out." He holds up his phone. It's true, we're at a steady 28, with reports of dropping lower. "They're predicting snow . . . a big one."

"You sound like a newbie," I say. "I'll believe it when I see it."

"It's snowing in Colorado," a cute girl at the bar interrupts. She holds up her phone so I can see what she's looking at. A park ranger in Mesa Verde is streaming video through his eyes, the flakes layering the cliff dwellings beneath a blanket of white. She blinks to another channel, and now there's a meteorology student at Colorado University, broadcasting his own weather report of *The Last Storm,* claiming the blizzard's moving toward Utah. She clicks off her phone and leans toward me. "I know you," she says.

"Oh yeah?"

"Mmhm, you're Ronnie Hawks. I used to watch you all the time."

When, I wonder—when you were six? Instead I just say thanks.

"You were crazy," she says. "Do you still ski like that?" I see Angie roll her eyes before she goes down the bar to refill a pitcher.

Her name's Chloe, she's from UC, and though it's been forever since anyone wanted to flirt about skiing, it feels good. I lean over the bar and tell her about heli-skiing the Himalayas, what it was like to drop down the face of a deathmaker. And Angie, who knows I've been alone all season, decides not only to let me flirt, but also tells me she'll close down tonight. "Go live out your never-ending adolescence," she says.

Chloe's staying at the Bear Creek Lodge with her folks, so we take the shuttle back to my apartment, which is a mess. The coffee table's covered in vintage ski magazines, broken-up dope, my vaporizer, and empty bottles of microbrew.

"Sorry about the mess," I say as she surveys the posters on the wall of snowboarders and half-pipes.

"It's fine. Kinda looks like my little brother's room."

I roll a joint for us, and we smoke on the couch and start making out before the thing's halfway burnt. Chloe's body reminds me how it'd once been my dream to grow old but keep hooking up with young fans. I lift off my shirt and show her my scars. "God," she says, "that's hot." Then she wraps her legs around me and I lift her off the couch, my back screaming, and carry her to the bedroom. She unbuckles my pants, kicks them down with her legs, and I strip off her tights.

"Hey," she says, stroking me through my boxers, "I really want you to fuck me . . . but I'm just wondering . . . do you have—?"

"Totally," I say. I reach over, open my drawer, and find a condom.

"Oh," she says when she sees the foil wrapper. "I mean, that's cool, but . . . actually . . . I was going to ask . . . do you have your contacts in?"

When I was running the circuit, girls always asked me to keep my contacts in so they could show their friends my feed the next day, prove they'd slept with me. But Angie hadn't wanted my followers watching, so we'd made it a point to take them out before we'd have sex. I'd gotten used to Angie, but now I remember the way other girls liked it. "Totally," I say, reaching for the contacts container next to my condoms. "I'll put them in for you."

"Um . . . I was kind of hoping you'd be up for wearing mine?"

"Huh?"

"I want to do a selfie. It's kind of a way I make money. I've got a channel where guys can watch me get fucked. Don't worry, it's totally cool, you won't be in it at all." I take a deep breath, have to remind myself that it's been a long time since I've been with a girl this young, before I agree. "Cool, thanks," she says. She props herself onto her elbows and takes out her contacts, extends them to me on the tips of her fingers like a peace sign. I take the lenses, feel the weird intimacy of placing her contacts against my eyes, and then I'm in her feed, watching the comments scroll along my peripheral vision as I look at her. *You're so fucking hot! God I'd fuck that ass. Hit me back *//bigdawg.*

"Look at what I'm doing to you," Chloe says as she pulls me from my boxers. And I do look for a second but then realize I'm on camera, so look back at her. "I'm going to fuck you so good," she moans, and stares deep into my eyes as she pulls me toward her.

THE TEMPERATURE STAYS low, and the next night Rick messages me: *Want to run blowers with Sunny tonight? Overtime pay.* Back in the day you had to be licensed to work the machines, but since the Thaw, working on a mountain means taking five jobs. I'm a bartender, line cook, blower mechanic, ski instructor, and a liftie when newbies don't show. So after working bar, I head out with Sunny on snowmobiles to make sure the blowers are functional. Two pumps are flooded by Devil's Ridge, and a blower at Lightning Bowl has a clogged nozzle. The pipeline corroded and flaked rust into the machine and there's only so much we can do, but we clear it out and it's shooting clean by the time we get it done.

It's past midnight by the time we pull onto the peak over Hidden Valley and lie back against the seats, watching the machines spray mist into the air. Sunny's brought a bowl, and we pass it back and forth, watching the water turn into snow below us. The sky's patched with clouds, a gap of stars here and there, but they're moving quickly, the air cold like I haven't felt in a long time.

"Can you believe it's over?" Sunny says and sparks the bowl. "No more boarding, no more nights like this. Should've gone to Dubai when we had the chance, snagged some lift jobs. You know how long those lists are?"

I do. It was the first jobsite I went to after we got the news we were closing. *Ski Dubai is no longer taking applications— all positions filled for the foreseeable future.* I take the bowl from him. "What are you planning to do for work?" I ask.

"Going to teach surf lessons in Kaua'i."

"Isn't that your summer job?"

"Full-time now."

"Wish I'd learned to surf."

"Never too late—come with me. My friend runs a dispensary; I'll talk to him, get you hooked up with a job selling bud."

I imagine myself on a beach somewhere, high every day, trying to learn a sport I'm no good at. It's an option, I guess. Probably better than trying to get a job bartending down in the valley where the list of applications is as long as Dubai. "Angie was talking about Brazil."

"You guys still a couple?"

"No. She just said she was heading down there to help build houses for people who lost it all. I was thinking I might go with her."

"You serious? I mean that's respectable of you, but you're telling me you'd be stoked doing that *instead* of surfing and smoking top-shelf bud?"

"I don't know," I admit, and decide not to say anything more about Brazil. I'm not even sure Angie would want me along. But I keep thinking if she'll take me with her, maybe something good could come out of it, for both of us.

A couple thick flakes land on our snowmobiles and against our parkas. "Shit, is that snow?" Sunny asks. We look up at the sky, and sure enough the clouds have moved in, the stars completely gone, and big flakes are coming down. "Sure is," I say in awe. I cover the bowl with my glove and spark the lighter. Besides the sound of crackling buds, there's nothing but the quiet of the mountains and the snowflakes falling against the slopes.

"It's going to be crowded tomorrow if this keeps up."

"Don't worry," I say, "by dawn it'll turn into chowder."

But by the time Sunny drops me off at the apartments, it's still snowing heavy, the streetlights a wild whir of slanted snow. The drifts are piling up on my porch when I brush my teeth, and come the alarm at seven, there's over two feet of fresh powder, our parking lot transformed into igloos where cars once were. "Holy shit," I say and have to go digging in my closet to find thermals.

It's all anyone can talk about on the radio. Mostly just hoots coming through. *Woo-hoo!* Sunny yells. *Powder, man, fucking powder!* And it doesn't let up, the snow keeps falling. It turns out most of the crew is AWOL. Zeke's abandoned the ski shop and Sunny's already shredding the slopes. Even Rick is nowhere to be found. For a moment I think about setting up the bar, then say fuck it, and abandon post as well. Let the fools who want free drinks steal what they can.

The mountain is speckled with skiers, the parking lot filling with new arrivals, and I can sense the itch to hike back country again, see the cliffs, feel my adrenaline spike. I take the quad over to Powder Ridge, and when I get off at the top,

I decide to hitch my skis over my shoulder and hike over the mountain, out of bounds. It's rough going, powder past my knees, my legs moaning as I climb.

On those nights when I wouldn't fast-forward, I'd sit watching my biography, studying the last moments of my mistake. In the video, the copter takes off and I see myself heading toward the cliff, my skis carving a big arc before I sail off the edge. You can already see how I'm falling the wrong way, my body too close to the mountain. Usually I could feel an imbalance in the dismount, had time to correct for the mistake, but when I hit that cliff I thought I knew exactly where I was landing. I remember those split seconds before my hip smashed against the rocks, my neck buckled back and my screens went blank. My followers were cheering in my feed. *We love you Hawks!* Emoji after emoji giving a thumbs-up and then, suddenly, screaming emojis, a skull and crossbones, all the OMGs. The last thing I saw was rock, like the mountain had hooked into my side and was corkscrewing me down its granite face, the sun twisting as I rode the mountain the whole way, my body rag-dolling down the fall line.

It's all coming back to me now as I cross onto the other side of the peak. Everyone's gone, there's just the white expanse of uncut powder and the quiet of falling snow. I can feel the old rush of conquering the mountain and what it was like to hit the bottom of the run unscathed. Down below me is nothing but pines and cliffs. Even if it's a suicide run, at least I'll be watched again.

I can feel my heart pounding, my breath short and ragged, the adrenaline filling me, and I understand that I'm not just taking one run and heading back to the bar to set up for lunch, and I sure as hell won't be asking Angie if I can go with her to South America; I'm going to make the greatest comeback video anyone has ever seen. I reach into my pocket and take out my contacts case, duck my head away from the snow, and put my tacts back in. "Hey there," I say to the world of potential followers, "You're all going to want to see this." Then I lower my goggles, letting my skis slide into unbroken snow, and lean into the fall line opening beneath me.

A BRIEF HISTORY OF THE
FAILED REVOLUTION

WHILE KROTSKY WASN'T the first to propose that the work at the Consciousness Institute was political rather than scientific, he was the most outspoken of the critics. In his essay *The Global Interface as Political Machine,* he argues, "If we see consciousness as belonging to an individual, in much the same way that we consider personality, free will, or even the notion of soul as his/her own possession, then we must concede that any technological intrusion, cybernetic or electronic, is a forcible one. As such, the individual should have a right to reject it."[1]

That private ownership of consciousness was Krotsky's main objection to the Global BrainWeb Interface certainly weakened his argument. For as Dksvoskny pointed out, if consciousness is claimed as private ownership, then "soon enough perfume, music, even the wind will be up for debate,

---

1. Krotsky, Samuel. "The Global Interface as Political Machine." *Cyber-Medical Journal* Vol XII (2028):19.

for are not all of these *consciousness-intruding* elements?"[2] Dksvoskny was thus the first to formally question what constituted proper objection to technological intrusion outside of the subjective like/dislike standards proposed by anti-interfacers. Ethics, he stated, was hardly the basis to reject a leap in human/computer intelligence, conceding that if, and only if, such an intrusion were dangerous (i.e., a stench so foul, it caused vomiting; a noise so loud, it produced deafness), then, indeed, prohibition would be up for debate.

The BrainWeb Interface, however, increased brain/computer function without any such violent intrusions. And while the initial test models complicated this due to their primitive designs (SkullCartridges, Internal DSL, VeinWiring, etc.) these prototypes were quickly replaced by the nonintrusive, marketplace models available from the construction of the Towers. The technology that allowed the web to function directly off bioenergetics rather than internal hardwiring, in short, its nonphysicality, invalidated the anti-interface objections.

Wittger, who separates behavior into internal-drive and external-drive behavior, sees the crux of the debate as residing in the misconception of consciousness as being purely word/thought based rather than word/thought/html based.

Who exactly gave anti-interfacers divine right to hold neural function under lock and key still remains a mystery to

---

2. Dksvoskny, Ludov. "Imprisoning the Wind: A Rebuttal of Krotskyism." *CyberMedical Journal* Vol XIII (2029): 28.

me. An antiquated notion of sovereign control of brain function is, in part, at fault. Religious dogma is probably more culpable (with its notions of spirit, reincarnation, ad infinitum). When religion established the intangible soul as a safe haven for consciousness, it compromised techno-logical evolution by creating a mind eternally hidden and impossible to access. The advance of Global Interface Technology has proven that the neuroscience of the early twenty-first century provided only a limited understanding of brain function. Human internal drive has had cybernetic interface at its disposal all along.[3]

Wittger proved that, in the same way electricity or grav-ity was present before its discovery, human cybernetic capa-bility preexisted the technology, and to deny this was to prove universal imbecility. Indeed, the short-lived attempts of anti-interfacers to remove themselves from the Global Streaming Network (ostriching, metal helmets, the Spelunk Architec-tural Movement) gave merit to the imbecility Wittger proph-esied. None of the gloom and doom that anti-interfacers warned about occurred, and while Smith attributes a rise in IDFD (Internal Drive Focus Disorder) and the proliferation of Interface Psychosis to the emergence of interfacing,[4] Bausch

3. Wittger, Ivan. "The Problem of God: Anti-interface Dogma vs. Sci-ence." *Tech. Quarterly* (2030): 86.
4. Smith references cases such as AISDD (Autoimmune Streaming Detachment Dysfunction) reported by the Center for Interface Monitoring,

& Cartz Pharmaceuticals has shown that these diseases were latent in the individual pre-Interface.[5]

Perhaps the more interesting argument posed by the anti-interface movement is Professor Schisberg's discussion of the collective unconscious. He suggests, "The intra-psychic phenomena noted by many since the advent of interfacing cannot simply be examined as conventional psychic phenomena. Current cases of Interface-synchronicity point to corporately chosen subject matter. The question this raises is whether the Interface is rewiring our collective unconscious to become corporate."[6] Insofar as this is an interesting philosophical argument, Schisberg's claims have held some sway. However, as Dunning observes, "The collective unconscious remains as much a mystery as life and death itself. Suggesting that the nature of mind is corporately

---

with symptoms including insomnia/verbal streaming/disconnect incapability/myopic-googling/etc. In his study *Off-Line Disturbances: A History of Interface Dysfunction,* Smith refers to a patient's inability to speak about anything but variations on casserole recipes as Chronic Googling, and uses this as a metaphor to examine nondysfunctional social behavior, stating that, "Even we, the supposed un-disturbed, still find it hard not to hum pop-up jingles, or assimilate interface ads into our speech, as is the case with the notorious adage, *Mega-fun!*"

5. Medical studies conducted by Bausch & Cartz Pharm. Inc. showed that up to 64 percent of newborns and 78 percent of individuals above the age of eighteen produced insufficient amounts of cyber-cerebral neurotonin to functionally navigate the Interface.

6. Schisberg, Douglas. "Unsettling Disturbances: A Study of Interface Synchronicity." *CyberMedical Journal* Vol XX (2031): 26.

controlled is as ridiculous as claiming the afterlife is politically influenced."[7]

The anti-interface movement, which initially rose in outward physical protest, has been quelled over the past decade, becoming decidedly academic in nature.[8] Krotsky himself, originally the most vocally supportive of the resistance, conceded that physical rebellion (i.e., Tower Terrorism, Interface scramblers, brain pirating) was ultimately pointless.

> Regardless of our consent, the Interface has reorganized the mental landscape and firmly established consciousness as public property. Through violence, defeat, and default, the resistance has been forced to create a final stronghold via the intellect itself. The emergence of university-level Interface Studies is the only fortuitous outcome of the failed revolution. Intelligence should henceforth be seen as a type of capital. Ideas, hypotheses, and arguments are the only assurance the individual still has of buying power in the marketplace of consciousness.[9]

---

7. Dunning, Glade. "Nature and Mind." *Proctor & Gamble Annual Report* (2030): 74c.

8. *The Anti-Interface Protests,* Portland, Oregon. militarystrikeonline.com 12 Sept 2032. <usgov.militarystrike-USarmy/234/sept2032/rightlobe.intf>

9. Krotsky, Samuel. *Afterthoughts on Revolution.* Chicago: Black Raven Press (2034): 226.

MIGRATION

SHE'S WEARING KNEE-HIGH boots and a skirt short enough to expose her thighs. She waits for the few lagging students to exit, then closes the door and crosses the room toward my desk. Something is different about her eyes today. At first I mistake it for the purple eyeliner until I notice flecks of green superimposed on her brown irises. Her nose is small and her lips are large, deep red, and enhanced. "Hi, Professor," she says, leaning against the edge of the table. "You were checking me out again, weren't you?"

"You caught me," I say.

"You want to do something about it?"

Through the small pane of glass, I see students filing past the classroom. "Here?" I ask.

She puts her lips by my ear and whispers, "Yes, Dad, right here. Don't you want this?" She stretches her bronzed hand in front of me and shows me the vagina on her palm. "I've got two other ones for you, Dad." Her lips are by my earlobe where I've created a very small penis to resemble an earring. "Why don't you try to find them all, Dad," she says. "Dad?"

"Dad!"

I take off my goggles. Max is in the doorway, wearing the white hockey mask he never removes. "Dad, I've been calling you for, like, five minutes."

Beneath my desk, the black rubber of my bodysuit is bulging, revealing the early stages of an erection. I peel off my headgear, place it by the computer, and turn awkwardly, keeping my legs hidden under the desk. "Don't interrupt me when I'm teaching."

"Your class ended ten minutes ago."

"*Six* minutes ago. Either way, wait till my door opens, and take off that mask when I'm talking to you."

My son grunts and drops his shoulders, a kind of inverse shrug. There was a time when the sound of my office door opening would bring the excited patter of his feet. Now I can hardly get him to stand near me. He lifts the hockey mask so it juts over his eyes like a visor, casting shadows onto his face. "There," he says. "Do we have a bike pump?"

"A what?"

"A bike pump."

He's sweating, his left hand is shaking, and his pupils are all over the place. The kids call it spinning, a misnomer. His eyes aren't spinning, they just keep flicking from side to side like televisions once did when their antennae were crooked. This isn't the time to start a fight with him, not while I'm still sitting in my bodysuit with a partial erection. "What in the world do you need a bike pump for?"

"I can't bike online, our connection's too slow."

"And?"

"I could use the bike I have."

"No. It's dangerous out there."

"Come on."

"I said no. End of discussion."

"*Fine!* I'll just be in my room killing zombies like I always am!" He flips down his hockey mask and slams the door behind him. Slasher-punk music starts up and the house is filled with guitars that sound like chain saws. Then the guitars give way to a drum solo from a programmed kit, which makes erratic and purposefully ill-timed beats. *Bapbapbap. Bapbapbap. Bapbapbap.* This isn't music.

My computer chimes: an instant message.

Where'd you go?

Sorry, I type, *family stuff. Can we meet online tonight? I can rent a hotel room. Ten o' clock?*

Want 2 fuck u in classroom.

I pause over the keys. *I can set up a site with a king bed. Jacuzzi?*

Nix. Classroom or nogo.

I let out a sigh. *Make it 11. The room's closed, but I can log us in.*

C-ya.

I log off and wonder what the hell I'm doing. If I were

smart, I'd pay an avatar for a night, rent a pre-made space, and not worry about sleeping with a student. Of course, then it wouldn't be Kira—which, I suppose, means I'm not yet too old to get excited by the forbidden. I remove my bodysuit, hang it over the back of the chair, and put on jeans and a T-shirt. Then I go see my wife in her office.

"I can't stand that fucking music," I say, closing the door behind me.

She turns away from her computer and lifts her goggles. "It's awful, isn't it? Come here and give me a kiss."

I cross the room and lean down toward her. The goggles are in the way, so our lips barely brush before we make a kissing sound. She puts her hand on mine, and I feel connected to her. Then I think about Max and the warmth frosts over. Ann feels the change right away. "What is it?"

"Max is on drugs again. His eyes were flickering and he said he wanted to go bicycling."

"You mean those bikes your parents gave us? That's ridiculous. We haven't been outside in years."

"I know. He's probably meeting someone to get drugs."

The reality of the situation leaves us silent. When we first had the suspicion Max was doing drugs, I'd snooped into his search history and stumbled onto one of the sites he'd visited. On the screen a red dot flashed, upper left-hand corner then lower right, blinking three times, large then tiny, before switching to blue. Simply following the dot with my eyes, I felt my mind unhinge. Colors bloomed on the back sides of my eyelids and I had the fleeting thought: *There are limitless hues within the human heart.* My fingers began tingling as though my veins were connected to a larger network of neurons crisscrossing cyberspace, and I had the sudden and inexplicable urge to double-click an object that didn't exist. I removed the goggles, my pupils spasming left, right, left, right, as the spectrum of colors receded into the eggshell of our bedroom walls. After that we put blocks on our home connections, but Max still managed to find a way around them.

"Well, he's here with us," Ann says. "And he's not going to leave without us knowing it." She's always been the rational one. She gives my hand a squeeze and extends her goggles. "I'm almost done with the Whole Foods account; tell me what you think."

Ann's landscaped their online corporate office with a carpet of green grass. Patches of violets and buttercups brighten the unused corners, and flat hovering stones create a staircase between the upper and lower levels. The floor-to-ceiling windows have been tinted so the light streaming through is the eternal hue of late afternoon: not too bright to squint, not too dim to read, a perfect radiance that highlights the natural colors of human skin. Outside, a tropical coastline spans the horizon, palm trees stretching over the waves.

"Hawaii?" I ask.

"Philippines."

"Nice touch." I take off the goggles. As stunning as Ann's

landscaping is, her work always depresses me. Her worlds make the white walls of our home seem all the more drab. We stenciled lilacs around the perimeter, but it really can't compare.

I cross the room and sit down on the office bed. Ann's got her goggles back on and is dragging and clicking her fingertips across the design pad. "So?" she asks from over her shoulder. "Did you do Kira today?"

"No," I admit. "We've got plans for tonight."

"What time?"

"Eleven."

"Maybe Rick can meet me then."

Rick is Ann's gardener, a muscular twenty-eight-year-old Latino avatar who sells her palm trees. She introduced me to him once while showing me the Whole Foods office. He was shirtless when I'd met him and was carrying a palm tree under his arm. He said, "What's up, bro?" as a greeting.

"You know he's probably some hairy guy in Kalamazoo, right?"

"And Kira's not?"

"Kira's definitely not," I answer, though I have no clue. I picture a balding middle-aged man sitting in an apartment, his floor littered with chips and Coke bottles as he crafts Kira's avatar. For all I know, my wife is right—the university no longer gives us gender, age, or birth names, just a class list based on my students' chosen identities. "Are you really okay with this?" I ask.

"Are you kidding? I've been okay from the start. You're the one who calls it cheating."

It's true. I'm from the generation who had hookups through Tinder and erased websites from browsers, a generation who, for a short while, still had time to be idealistic about what the future held. Ann's eight years younger; her generation lost their online virginity in middle school.

"Come on," Ann says, "it's going to be fun. We'll be next to each other when we get off."

"Explain to me again how this isn't cheating?"

Ann takes off her headset and crosses the room to sit by me. "They're just avatars," she says and kisses me. It feels good. Even though real lips can't bring you to orgasm, there's something nice about them all the same. We kiss again, a short one this time; then Ann returns to her work, and I go back down the hallway—past Max's music of groaning car engines and screeching violins—to my office. I put my body-suit back on for a walk.

Ann created *Autumn* for us when Max was five, a Father's Day gift. As a little boy, Max and I would walk the landscape together, he in his bodysuit and I in mine, but nowadays I just bring up a saved avatar of Max and reach down to take his hand. The air is crisp and startling, a day that hints toward the coming winter. The leaves have begun turning, and they fall from large oaks, covering the ground in yellow and orange.

"Hi, Daddy," Max says. The simulator gives his child's sweetness a disturbing digital timbre, but it's close enough.

"Hey," I say and squeeze his hand. Above us, a couple planes cut white trails across the sky, and I hold my son's hand as we step from the sidewalk into a sea of golden leaves.

※

MAX WEARS HIS hockey mask through dinner. He lifts it only to take bites of the lemongrass tilapia Ann has prepared. We've asked him to take the mask off when we eat. We've punished him, grounded him, taken away his video-game time, but there's no victory in having a mask-less boy who hates us. So, Ann and I talk to each other while our son silently tends goal at the end of the table. The mask isn't his invention. Some teenager somewhere found their grandparents' B-grade horror films and decided the mask was the new vogue for angry anti-tech youth. Indeed, the mask is chilling. The hard, emotionless white fiberglass covers our son's features, and the hollow, perpetually sunken eyes create a furious expression. The triangles of red above the cheeks resemble streaks of blood. When you add in his clothing—a costume based entirely on either hazmat suits or straitjackets—our son looks essentially like a mass murderer.

It pains Ann and me to see Max like this, knowing that beneath the darkness of the mask his eyes are still spinning, his mind is high on cybernetics, and his heart is full of some pain neither of us understands. Max wasn't always like this. Until he was eleven, he was a sweet child with a downy head of hair and cheeks that lifted in smiles. He played online games like *Club Koala,* where he clung to eucalyptus trees and traded in bamboo shoots for fur upgrades. Then he entered middle school. We'd bought his school avatar a *Club Koala* shirt. The other students made fun of him, and a group of tech-savvy assholes hacked into his *Club Koala* account and spray-painted his bear pink. They made his koala say obscene things to the other bears, which left Max permanently expelled from the site. That's when he bought the hockey mask and straitjacket and teamed up with the slasher-punk kids at school, a group that refuses to streamline their avatars. They wear patches that read NO DIFFERENCE! and appear online in the same gruesome costumes they wear at home.

"I'm done eating," Max says. "Can I be excused?"

We let him leave the table, even though Ann and I are only halfway through our fish, and Max disappears upstairs.

"That was pleasant," Ann says. Machine-gun noises cut her off, followed by the sound of jackhammers on a keyboard.

"Max!" I yell. No answer. "Max!"

"What?"

"Turn it down. And it's going off in half an hour."

His reply is to slam the door, but the music does lower.

Ann washes the dishes and I order another shipment of groceries. Beets, milk, honey; Chesapeake mussels are on sale. I click them into my cart. I think of the people working out there, transporting seafood across the country, driving mile after mile of empty highways. There are weekly reports of truck attacks by refugees living outside. I click my cart and check out.

By ten the slasher-punk is turned off, and by a quarter to eleven Max is asleep. The house is quiet again. I sit on our bed as Ann gets her equipment ready. She pulls off her sweater, then unhooks her bra. Her body looks good. It's not as slim as her avatar. Around the hips she's gained some weight but, then again, so have I. She's at least better at going to online yoga.

I try to mentally prepare myself for Kira, but all I can think about is how Ann and I have a good love life. After fifteen years of marriage we still manage to have sex with each other's avatars two to three times a week. We've swapped genders, created a third programmed avatar to have three-ways with, placed genitalia on every inch of our bodies and had simultaneous multiple-appendage orgasms. It's not for a lack of experimentation. If that were the case, Ann could design a version of herself that looks exactly like Kira. But somehow that's not the same. Ann shifts her hips back and forth to slip out of her jeans, then pulls down her panties. I reach out and place my hand against her legs. Her skin feels soft.

"Are you sure you want to do this?" I ask.

"Yeah, baby." She steps into her suit and pulls the zipper up past her navel.

"You look hot," I say.

"You do, too," she says, pointing at my boxers. "Aren't you going to get dressed?" She pulls on her head mask and lowers her goggles.

"I'll be right there." I remove my boxers, slip my bare legs into my suit, secure my penis in the catheter, then zip in. The clock by the bed reads 10:57. I put on my mask and goggles and lie down next to Ann.

"I'm right here," she says, taking my hand.

Then we log on.

⁂

KIRA IS WAITING for me by the door of the classroom. Her hair is dark brown tonight, and it falls past her shoulders, loose and wild against her trench coat, in constant motion, as though blown by a breeze. She lifts a hand to her face and brushes the hair from her eyes.

"Hey, there," she says. She places her hand behind my neck and pulls me toward her, our tongues rubbing across each other's lip receptors again and again. I unlock the door, and once inside, Kira pushes me against it, closing the door behind us. My shirt is already bulging and Kira rubs her hand along the buttons, then rips the collar around my shoulders, exposing the erection in the middle of my chest.

"Get on the desk," she says.

She unties her own trench coat, and in the dim light of the room I see the vagina beneath her right breast. She places her rib cage against mine. "Oh, God," I say as she pushes me inside and begins to rock. I take her hand, looking for the vagina on her palm.

"Not there anymore," she says, grinding back and forth.

"What did you do with it?"

"I've got something better for you." She pulls her hair aside to reveal the puckered lips on the side of her throat.

"You're so beautiful," I say, and push my fingers into her neck. Already I can feel the hum in her body. She grabs the back of my head and pulls me toward her. "You've got one, too, don't you?"

"Yes," I say, moving my fingers in and out of her neck.

"I want it," Kira says, her voice suddenly harsher. "Tell me where it is."

"My leg."

Kira unbuttons my pants and yanks them around my knees, fully exposing the vulva on my right thigh. She lifts her leg from the floor, her own erection protruding from her kneecap, and pushes into me. She grunts, lifts her leg into a horse kick, and drives her knee down again. I moan.

"Don't stop fucking me," she says. I push my fingers deeper into her neck as she jackhammers her knee into me. She's rocking up and down, her leg kicking back and forth, her neck nodding in unison as her rib cage begins shaking. "Keep going!" And I want to, but she has me pinned against the desk and I can barely lift my leg. "This is it!" she yells. Her neck clenches tightly around my fingers and her rib cage spasms as she collapses on top of me. Then her weight is gone, her avatar popping from above with the sound of a computer logging off. The room is quiet, the desks and chairs all lined up in perfect rows, and the moon outside casts a silver light across the floor. I'm alone on my desk, my shirt torn, the silk ruined, and my pants are around my ankles. I pull my trousers back on and try to button my ruined shirt—it's no use—then I slide off the desk and shut down the classroom.

My wife is still lying on the bed beside me. Her lips are parted and she's letting out a slow moan. I take a couple breaths, staring at the lilacs stenciled around the ceiling. I count them: twenty-one . . . twenty-two . . . twenty-three . . . I tap my wife's shoulder. "Hey?" I say. There's no response, except her lips open slightly wider. "Hey," I say again, but she's too far gone.

What I want to do is lie down with Ann, hold her, and go to sleep. But that's not what's happening. She's kicking her foot up and down on the bed with no indication of stopping anytime soon. I think about logging back on and finishing myself off with a programmed avatar, but it feels too pathetic. So, I strip off my headgear and peel down the bodysuit, my leg hairs sticking to the rubber as I remove it. Then I go to the bathroom and turn on the water. In the mirror, my pupils are dilated as though in shock and my hands are shaking. I sit on the toilet and take a deep breath. The tiles are yellow beneath my bare feet, and my body smells sour from the suit. In the other room, I hear a drawn-out moan. There's nothing to do except log on, watch something on Virtuview, check my email, or buy my avatar a new shirt—none of which sounds interesting. So, I take a shower. Then I put on my robe, close the bedroom door behind me, and head downstairs to find something to eat.

Halfway down the stairs, I hear a thump. I freeze on the last carpeted step. There's the strained silence of someone trying to be quiet, then a tentative squeak starts up, growing quicker. I'm thinking of instant messaging the police when I recognize the sound.

Max is crouched by the bicycles in our garage. He's still in his flannel pajamas, and his hockey mask is up over his head. Above him, the frosted bulb casts a bleak light onto our car, which is buried beneath boxes labeled CHRISTMAS ORNA-MENTS and MAX'S BABY CLOTHES.

"What are you doing?" I ask.

There's a clatter of handlebars as he gets to his feet, trying to hide the pump behind his back. "Nothing," he says. He's forgotten to pull his mask down, but now he remembers and lowers it.

"Show me what's behind your back."

Max brings out the pump. "I found it."

"You were going bicycling at this hour?"

"No," Max says. "Seriously, Dad, I wasn't. I just wanted to get my bike ready. You know, like to go riding after school or something."

I don't know what to say. Seeing him standing there in

his flannel pajamas, it sure doesn't look like he's planning on going anywhere. Still, none of this makes any sense. "Max, tell me what's going on."

"Nothing," he says. "All I want to do is go biking."

"Don't lie to me."

"I'm not lying."

"Where were you going?"

"Nowhere!"

"To get drugs?"

"No!" he yells. "God, you never leave me alone!" He throws the aluminum pump to the ground, where it clatters hollowly.

"Hey!" I grab his arm. It's the first time I've touched my son in months, and the shock of his skin beneath mine suddenly reminds me of what it was like to hold him as a child. My voice catches. I release my grip and he's out the door, his footfalls echoing through the kitchen and up the stairs. His bicycle sits, ready for escape, next to my own deflated bicycle. It's only as I take the bike pump and begin to inflate my own tires that I think to exhale.

❊

THE NEXT MORNING feels strange. We do our usual routine, get up, shower, eat cereal with Max, but I don't feel connected to any of it. I stack the dishes in the dishwasher and think of Kira's knee inside me. Max logs in to school and we close his door.

"Can we talk?" Ann says.

"Not now, I've got office hours."

"You promised we'd talk in the morning. Something's wrong, I can tell."

"Nothing's wrong."

Ann doesn't say anything; she just stands there, an arm's reach from me, looking like a stranger. "I promise we'll talk later," I say and turn, leaving her in the hallway as I escape to my office.

The system logs me on without any Departmental Message pop-ups. My inbox is full of junk mail, a virtual greeting card from my mother, and a couple emails from students asking about the essay that's due in two hours. I hang around my office, waiting for students to show up. I gaze out the window, flip through the Seven Wonders of the World, and think about Kira. There's a reality wherein Kira and I are a couple, a world where I'm eternally thirty, without a wife who's quickly aging or a son on drugs. I could move out, get my own apartment, live a new life, alone and happy with a thousand avatar lovers.

When it's time for class, the students arrive, but I'm waiting to see Kira. Her seat is empty when the bell rings, so I wait a couple minutes longer, and then, with a sigh, begin teaching. I'm halfway into my lecture on Joyce's "The Dead" when Ann starts shaking my body. I excuse myself and raise my goggles.

"I'm in the middle of class," I say.

"The garage door just opened."

"What?" I ask, pulling my goggles completely off.

"Max is outside!"

"Shit!" I dismiss class and log off to find my son.

※

MAX'S BIKE IS gone. The garage is open on its hinges, letting in the blinding glare of the world and a cold blast of wind that cuts through my shirt.

"I'm going after him," I say and cross the garage to my bicycle. I raise the kickstand and walk the bike to the edge of our garage.

"You need a jacket; it's freezing out there." Ann pulls boxes off our car and onto the ground. I hear something shatter in our Christmas box. She opens a large box that says WINTER GIVE-AWAY and yanks the puffy sleeve of an old coat I haven't seen in years.

"Be careful," Ann says, and then I'm off, pedaling away from our house, my tires crunching the salted road and echoing across the concrete of our subdivision. Out here all the houses look abandoned. The vinyl sides are yellowed and the blinds are drawn. Their front yards, like ours, are completely overgrown: high grasses, stalky and dry, rustle in the wind that blows down from the rooftops. The cold sucks the blue from the sky, deadens sound, and makes the streets desolate. I pedal wobbly along our road, turn down the first intersection, then the next, a right, followed by a left, surrounded by nothing but darkened windows and sidewalks. I push harder against the pedals, sweeping the empty streets for my son. My breathing becomes a labored rasp, my legs ache, and it's only when I stop the bicycle to catch my breath that I hear the muted sound of tires between the houses. I follow the sound down the street, turning on another street, another, and then out past the houses, leaving our subdivision for the long flatlands between the suburbs and the abandoned shopping plaza on the horizon. Far ahead, I can see Max's outline.

Vacant car dealerships lie fallow by the long stretch of the four-lane road as I huff to keep up with him, my knuckles purple from the cold. A truck rumbles past, delivering groceries. Ten minutes, fifteen. I am far behind my son by the time he reaches the abandoned plaza. I pull off the road, behind an overgrown pine by the entrance, and scan the lot for Max's drug dealer.

Max slaloms between the metal lampposts, stopping by the tinted doors of the entrance to the mall. He cups his hands against the glass and looks inside. Then he gets back on his bike and swoops around the side of the building. By the jagged shards of a smashed Toys"R"Us window, Max dismounts and leans his bicycle against the brick wall. He removes his goalie mask and hangs it on the handlebars, then digs around in his coat pocket and pulls out a green orb. From this distance I can't make out what the object is, consider that it may be some sort of new drug, until he throws it.

The tennis ball rebounds on the concrete with a delayed echo. Max catches it, then throws it again. He doesn't seem to be looking for anyone; he's simply throwing the ball and catching it, throwing it and catching it. A couple of times the ball hits a cracked patch of concrete and rebounds crookedly, rolling across the blacktop, but otherwise it's the same monotony for five minutes, ten minutes, a quarter of an hour.

The day is dying around us. Soon the sun will be gone, the roads dark. I roll my bike from behind the pine and enter the open expanse of Parking Lot B, where Max is playing. He doesn't see me until I'm halfway toward him, and when he does, he jumps.

"Max," I call. He stands frozen, holding the ball, and it's only when I'm within three parking lot rows from him that he retreats to his bicycle to get his mask on.

"What are you doing here?" I ask.

"Nothing."

"I saw you throwing the ball. What was that for?"

"Just for fun," he says, stuffing the ball into his jacket pocket.

"Take your mask off."

He lifts the mask up like a visor.

"All the way. I want to see your face."

He glares at me, tries to look angry, but the oddity of being out here together in the cold has affected him and I can see his fear. He reluctantly lifts off his mask. "There, you happy?"

All the time I was following him, I imagined myself yelling when we got to this point. I envisioned a fistfight with a slasher-punk drug dealer. Now all I feel is the smallness of our bodies and a palpable loneliness—the two of us lost in this enormous plaza. "No, I'm not happy," I say, and lean my bike against his. "You know it's dangerous coming out here like this, don't you?"

"What's dangerous about it?"

"You don't know who could be out here."

Max gives an ugly laugh. "Right," he says. "Look at all the people."

"Don't be sarcastic. There *could* be people out here. Their tents could be anywhere. Please . . . I just want to know what you're doing here."

Max doesn't respond. He looks down at the ground and kicks a loose chunk of blacktop with his combat boot, breaking it in half with his heel. "Don't you ever feel like things are boring?" he finally says. He looks at me. "Like colors get boring?"

I understand him better than he knows. In those brief moments when I'd been watching the flickering dot, I, too, had seen long-forgotten colors: the muted yellows of winter grass, the brown of tree bark, the rich black of earth. "What about *Deathworld*?" I ask.

"*Deathworld* is boring. You beat a hundred zombies, get a golden skeleton bone, and save the girl that the zombies kidnapped. I used to be excited about that, but now it's just like, great, I get to save this girl and make out with her for the hundredth time."

"They let you make out with those girls?"

"If you know the codes."

I look at my son. The sunlight highlights the few pale freckles on his cheekbones. His hair is in bangs around his face. He looks much more like a young man than the boy I remember. "You know, you're a good-looking kid."

"No, I'm not."

"Without the mask, you'd have a lot of girls interested in you."

"Nobody wants me with or without the mask. All they want is some fake avatar dude with a six-pack and three dicks."

I have no idea how to respond; Max just described my own avatar. I let out a long slow breath. "I guess I don't know how you meet girls nowadays," I say.

"You don't *meet* girls, just their avatars. It's stupid. Soon everybody's going to stop having kids and we'll all just die. Did you ever think about that?"

The truth is, I've ignored this fact. I've wanted to think that Max will go to college online, that we'll help him find a room for rent somewhere nearby, that he'll meet someone in one of his courses, fall in love, have kids one day. I've envisioned myself as a grandparent from time to time. For the first time I realize how far that vision is from reality. I look at the smashed Toys"R"Us window. "Max, you're not in trouble, but I don't get it. Why are you here?"

Max is quiet, debating what to tell me. He breaks up more of the blacktop, kicking it into the parking lot. Finally he looks up. "What is this place, anyway?"

"You used to have to come here to get stuff, shop for groceries, buy clothing."

"*Really?* Was it fun?"

I look at the empty toy store, where the rusted racks stand like skeletons in the windows, and I have a brief flash of what the place once looked like: the aisles of stuffed animals, dirt bikes, and video games, glossy beneath the lights. We watched these stores wither away, the shelves empty, the customers vanish, until the mall became a wasteland of dollar stores and Indian grocers. It's easy to forget what things were like. "It was nice in its own way," I say.

Max looks up at me. "You know, whenever I play Tennis, the ball always bounces smoothly and makes the same sound. But that's not what happens in real life. It bounces differently."

"But this isn't playing Tennis. You need another person."

"Yeah, I know that, but what else am I supposed to do?"

"I don't know, but this isn't the way to—"

"I want to be outside. I want to ride my bike."

"Okay," I say, putting up my hands. "I get it."

Positioned as we are, looking at one another, we don't

notice the man until he moves. He's at the far end of Lot C, a dark, skinny shadow of a man clearly facing us. It looks as if he's wearing some sort of jacket.

"Dad, who is that?"

"I don't know." The man makes a movement in our direction. "Come on," I say, "let's get out of here."

Max and I hurry onto our bicycles, looking over our shoulders. Behind us, the man has stopped and is deathly still. He raises a hand as he watches us go, as though waving. Then the buildings swallow him and we're back on the roads, where a couple trucks are still making deliveries. We pull far into the shoulder and they roar past. We both keep looking behind us as we ride, but the man from the mall is long gone. The sun has disappeared, and high above, purple spreads across the light blue, and the first stars push their way through the sky. There are a few wisps of clouds, and snowflakes have started to fall, laying themselves softly on the roads and sidewalks. My hands feel frozen on the handlebars. I bring one at a time up to my lips and blow hot air across the knuckles to warm them, my fingers burning with the blood beneath.

We're a couple blocks from home when we see them. Max's brakes screech and his tires scratch against the salt as he comes to a stop. I, too, am caught by surprise and break quickly, coming to a whining halt. There must be at least a hundred of them, the herd stretching all the way from the front lawn on the east to the kitty-cornered marsh across the street. The deer stand at attention, their necks raised, their ears extended, every muscle rigid beneath their fur. A couple in the back step quietly to gain a better view of us, their long brown snouts breathing small clouds into the falling darkness.

Max puts his foot down onto the ground and steps off his bicycle. "Wow," he whispers.

"I know," I whisper back.

The world is quiet except for the hooves on the concrete and Max's breathing. Between the jigsaw of houses, another herd is migrating past the rotten swing set of an English Tudor. Above us, a V of birds crosses the sky, their honking close. I shut my eyes and imagine the grid of streets where my son and I stand, visualize beyond to our house where Ann is waiting for us, alone and worried, and farther still, far beyond our subdivision, to where the geese head toward warmth and herds make their way beneath the arc of evening sky. I want to tell Max that I love him; that he'll always be my son; that somehow everything will be okay again. But maybe that's too far from the truth. So, instead, I put my arm around him, and we stand together in the falling snow, watching the deer return to their migration.

THE PYRAMID AND THE ASS

ON THE EVENING when most of the civilized world was watching the Oscars on Innervision, Douglas Duncage, Ninth Incarnation, was having trouble enjoying the glamour. He sat on a leather couch in his Manhattan penthouse, sucking a Keebler Frozie Mocha, watching Natasha Smoker, Sixth Incarnation, receive her award. Her kimono fluttered in his vision, soothing his retinal sensors with silk. Innereye's color loss was mitigated by its sensitivity to texture, a small trade-off. Douglas felt the jolt of weight as Natasha Smoker's fingers wrapped around the award. Satellite impulses triggered the release of serotonin, and his eyes welled with tears. Her performance in *Noah's Ark* had been phenomenal; everyone had cried when she rescued the baby gorilla from the rain.

When the commercials appeared, Douglas focused his internal mouse, blinked his right eye to click the mute button, and activated his parietal lobe to open his eyemail. Superimposed over the commercials came the bright white of his inbox folder. He'd received seventeen new eyemails since the last commercial break. Over half were work related; three were in response to his EyeDate profile; and four were from Americannewswatch.com. The news was grim. A group of radical Buddhist terrorists, known as the Sword of Transcendental Wisdom, had kidnapped an ecotour of Americans in Tibet. On a televised broadcast, the Dalai Lama denied responsibility for the kidnappings, once again condemning Soul Co. "The use of laser technology has corrupted reincarnation for profit and disrupted the natural balance of life and death," he declared.

Fucking Buddhists, Douglas thought as he mentally scrolled down the page. It was the fifth kidnapping this month and Douglas knew enough about Buddhist terrorists to predict the outcome. Chips would be pulled from spinal cords, eyescreens would be sliced open, and the tourists would never be seen again.

Being kidnapped by Buddhist terrorists was Douglas's worst fear, and he full-heartedly approved of George W. Bush, Tenth Incarnation's, declaration of war on Tibet. Unfortunately, the Dalai Lama had escaped into the Himalayas and was now holed up in some cave, from where he sporadically broadcast televised screeds against America. If only they'd nuke the Dalai Lama; nuke Bush's critics with him. He knew their liberal discourse all too well: Bush shouldn't be permitted to be reelected for the nineteenth time just because he was in a new body; America was only in Tibet for the Himalayan quartz crystals; the U.S. government had helped fund the Sword of Transcendental Wisdom in exchange for reincarnation info; yadda, yadda. The sooner Tibet became a U.S. protectorate like Syria and Iceland, the sooner there'd be peace.

Douglas blinked off the news report and checked the response to his EyeDate profile. *Hi there, sexy. You sound high-tech. You want to meet later tonight? I get off work at ten. Blink me. K-5478.* It sounded promising. Douglas checked the clock at the bottom of his vision. There was still time to ogle some Innernet ass before getting in contact with K-5478.

Since the Personal Privacy Act had been passed, the number of online ass sites had greatly diminished. There were, however, still a couple of ass links available. Among these were Asian-male/female-ass.com, African-male/female-ass .com, and the somewhat troubling Buddhist-male/female -ass.com. This last one was certainly tempting. Douglas longed to see what terrorist asses looked like. He imagined them puckered and wrinkled from meditating all day.

Whether Buddhist asses were puckered or wrinkled would remain a mystery for, as far as Douglas was concerned, that site was off-limits. There were rumors that Buddhist-ass had been set up by the U.S. government to monitor national security threats. To log on would be to mark every file of his soul as a terrorist. No thank you. He had no interest in joining the detainees in the Virgin Islands. Douglas mentally typed in Whitefemaleass.com instead. Within seconds a mountain of pure ass filled his eyes: two round mounds, not a hair on them, with a glorious crack running between the buttocks.

As Douglas admired the perfection of the ass, the awful feeling reemerged. It was a pain he'd been suffering over the past year, and one that came with a very specific thought. *I don't feel like myself.* The thought was particularly disturbing because there was, technically, nothing wrong with him. He was thirty-five, had accumulated enough credits over his incarnations to live luxuriously, had recently upgraded his eye-drive, and just last week had downloaded the latest version of Innercourse 4.0. What then could possibly make him feel *not* like himself? All the same, the feeling was there. And this feeling was sparked by the fact that the white ass in his vision evoked a tingling sensation in his groin, not altogether unpleasant but foreign. Back in his second incarnation he might've worried about his appendix, but they'd removed that organ from his cloned body incarnations ago. In addition, ever since procreation had become obsolete, erogenous nerve impulses had been scrambled. Douglas's fear was, for this reason, unfounded.

Yet there was the sensation again. A warm, maddening heat that made Douglas want to rub his belly against the carpeting, pull his pants up and down, and grind his ass against a wall. He squirmed on the couch uncomfortably, sweating as though he'd been having Innercourse. Douglas decided to schedule a lab technician checkup when he got back from his business trip. Perhaps there was something wrong with his microchip, some misfiring of synapses. Worse yet—and he really didn't want to consider this—perhaps he'd contracted a virus.

Douglas checked the clock: 10:14. K-5478 would be off work by now. He blinked off Whitefemaleass.com, activated VirusRub28, logged on to EyeDate, and sent K-5478 an instant blink. Within seconds she blinked Douglas back. "Hi there, D-6701, was wondering when you'd blink me."

"Wanted to blink you sooner, but you were working."

"If we get to know each other, I might be up for you blinking me at work."

"Why don't you tell me a little about yourself."

"I'm tall, skinny, have nice hair, and a really great ass." The last four words scrolled across Douglas's vision seductively.

"Oh yeah? I like asses."

"Me, too. What about you? What system do you run?"

"Only the best: Eyedoc78, full brain-cell drive."

"Hmm . . . you must make a lot of money."

"I don't do bad," Douglas blinked, pausing for a moment before making his move. "Are we compatible?"

"Mmm-hmm. Why? Can't you feel this?"

Douglas's synapses fired as K-5478 tested his system with

a packet. There was an immediate release of dopamine as Douglas's chip warmed up. "Oooh, I can feel that. Go ahead and do that again."

"You like that? How about this?"

"Oh yeah," Douglas blinked. He used his occipital lobe to send off a long download from his hard drive.

"Mmm, I love it when you send me slow downloads. Oooh, God, it's taking so fucking long to download!" As the words scrolled across Douglas's vision, a large file imported into his brain. He leaned back into the couch, head sinking into the leather, as he transferred another large file to her.

"Oh, God, give me another. Go ahead, my system can take it."

He gave her a couple terabytes.

"Mmm . . . fuck yes. Keep going. Don't stop."

Douglas hadn't meant to stop, but he'd mis-blinked and turned Innervision back on. On the screen Brad Pitt, Tenth Incarnation, was pitching Soul Co. *Suspend your soul in your own personal quartz crystal till your NewSelf is ready for reincarnation! Heaven can wait, till then there's Soul Co.*—Douglas blinked off the commercial. "Can you take a torrent file?"

"Ohhhh, baby, I'm a torrent player," the words moaned. Douglas sent off the file.

"Mmmm, two can play at that game."

Douglas felt his brain struggling to download the full capacity of the torrent file K-5478 sent him. "You're getting my system so hot!" he blinked, trying hard not to overheat. His hands clawed into the couch as he struggled to type "Yeslh!" And now she was sending him file after file. As one file disappeared, another rode in behind with rhythmic succession. Downloads tumbled atop one another, opening and downloading, and he kept his internal eye on the mouse, scrolling and clicking, scrolling and clicking.

"Oh m;y Goddd, these files just keep opening and opekning. You're ducking beutful," she mistyped.

"You're so fixking hort!" he trembled to think, and then his chip was buzzing with the electronic hum that comes in those magnificent seconds before all Innernet vision goes blank. "Gjdk! Gpd! GFOD!" he chanted, and she joined him, "Gjdi, Gid, GODu!" He hung on, sending off another file, and another, his screen vibrating, the hourglass turning back and forth, and as he received one last file, he sent off a final download with numerous attachments.

"Godalkdjj;lD;oiuaelmmm . . ." came the response.

"ASOLAKERJL;ENDL.CHKLE;N!!!" Douglas managed, his eyescreens flickering as he slid back against the couch. Slowly, his system rebooted itself, whirring beneath his skin. A few words landed on his eyescreens.

"Thanks, D-6701. Blink me again sometime."

"Sure will, K-5478," he blinked and logged off.

※

INNERCOURSE HAD BEEN good that evening, and that, along with the emotional effects of the Oscars, left Douglas feeling altogether exhausted as he curled into bed and pulled the comforters around him. Douglas felt so tired that he decided not to download his dose of Seconal, and it was due to this that he had another of the unusual dreams, which had been plaguing him for the past year.

He dreamt of the woman again. They were standing on top of a large temple. He was placing the last stone into the top of the monument when he saw her. The stone slipped and fell by his feet. "They're coming," she said. Far below, the city blinked neon into the night. Large signs extended from the jungle of streets and houses, the glowing arches of an *M* lighting the urban landscape. Then he saw the dark bodies of tanks, and choppers cut the air. "We didn't make it!" the woman said. From below a voice yelled, *"Fire!"* A mortar shell exploded, bricks shattered, and white rubble rained down around them. The woman took his palms and folded them over his abdomen. "This is how you remember your memories. You've got to remember who you are. Remember why you left and find us. We're going to build the temple again."

One of the helicopters dropped explosives. The walls split open, and the temple crumbled beneath him. As Douglas fell, the outline of the woman, standing far above him, receded into darkness.

❋

DOUGLAS AWOKE, DEEPLY shaken, to a lovely May morning.
This would be the last time he went to bed without Seconal,
he promised himself. He took a shower, got dressed, and
fixed himself a bowl of Keebler Puffy Treats. He sat at his
kitchen table, eating the cereal, and scrolled through his eyemails. There was an eyemail from Phillip Monto, Ninth Incarnation, the meet-and-greet courier that Douglas was flying
in to connect with. The eyemail invited him out for dinner
and drinks that evening, courtesy of Soul Co.'s Denver Division. There would be a Hummer waiting for him when he
arrived. Douglas checked his personal eyemails. There were
a couple responses to his EyeDate profile and then another
series of upsetting messages from Americannewswatch.com.
The Dalai Lama had issued a new speech.

"America tries to control life because they have no knowledge of their own souls. Not until America accepts the Bardo
realms of reincarnation will they know peace. Soul Co.'s
mission has disturbed the karmic laws of rebirth and—"
Enough. Douglas blinked off the broadcast, put his bowl in
the sink, and headed out of his apartment.

Outside there wasn't a cloud in the sky and the heavens
were a magnificent white. Douglas felt happy. Of Innernet's
three color preferences, white, black, or gray, Douglas liked
white best. Douglas had turned on his eyetunes early that

morning, and as he walked toward his Hummer everything was in harmony with the music pulsing through his brain. The Hummers cued up mechanically at intersections, allowing other Hummers to motor past. Then those Hummers stopped and other Hummers rolled through in perfect playlist synchronicity. Across the street, a city worker scrubbed a wall, removing the graffiti outline of a pyramid, in time to the music. Even the pigeons that fussed about the concrete seemed tuned in.

Douglas got to his Hummer and passed his wrist over the handle. The door unlocked and Douglas climbed into the driver's seat. He right-blinked the Hummer icon in the lower left of his vision, scrolled down his destination list, and left-blinked OFFICE. The Hummer started up and backed out of the spot, electronically signaling the other vehicles to allow his exit.

A number of other workers arrived at Soul Co.'s Upper Manhattan Office at the same time as Douglas. They piled into the elevator and stood listening to their eyetunes as the elevator rocketed toward the apex of the tower. Douglas's ears began ringing. He turned down his music. "Hello?" he said aloud.

"Hey there, Doug, just making sure you're on your way in."

"In the elevator right now. The crystals set to go?"

"On my desk and waiting."

"Great. See you in less than a minute."

"Righto," the boss said, and the connection went dead.

✺

THE BRIEFCASE WAS made of white titanium and was filled with the crystals of fifty-seven souls. It felt heavy in Douglas's hand. His boss, a stout man in a white suit, sat behind a white desk. Behind him, through the floor-to-ceiling windows, the towers of Manhattan rose in white peaks.

"You all right today?" the boss asked. "You look like shit."

"Skipped my Seconal dose and slept awful."

The boss grunted. "Look, you've got fifty-seven souls there. I recommended you for this transport because you're the best courier we've got for a job this size. In other words, I can't have you falling asleep on the plane."

"Don't worry, I'm awake."

"You don't look very awake to me. You got any Alertin?"

"I can order some."

"Here, take these," the boss said and blinked. Douglas saw two attachments for Alertin arrive in his inbox. "Use one now; the other one's if you feel like you need it later. We can't have you dozing off with a shipment like that."

Douglas downloaded one of the Alertins. It was like a strong cup of coffee to his synapses. "Thanks," he said.

"Hey, only the best for the best," the boss said and winked. Checking his fucking eyemail while he talks to me, Douglas thought. "Have a good trip," the boss said. "And don't look at too many asses while you're out there."

✻

WHY WAS IT that no matter how advanced technology got, air travel still remained in the Space Age? Douglas pondered this question as he stood on yet another line taking off his shoes and unbuttoning his shirt. Ahead of him, a woman in a white brassiere stood in a small cubicle getting scanned for electronic data. Douglas put his clothes on the conveyer belt and walked bare-chested into the booth.

His direct flight had been canceled, and he'd been bumped to a partner airline that had a flight to Denver with connections through Philly, Minneapolis, and Chicago. Unfortunately the first leg to Philly was delayed, forcing him to miss his flight in Minneapolis and catch a commuter to Chicago. The sun was setting when Douglas finally boarded the Chicago flight to Denver. Though the company had booked business class, his standby status bumped him back to economy. He eyemailed Phillip Monto to say he was delayed. *No problem,* the eyemail came back, *Grab a bite on the plane and we'll make it after-dinner cocktails instead.*

Innernet activity was prohibited on all flights and so Douglas, bored, looked out his window. Along the tarmac, men in white jumpsuits waved white neon sticks at incoming planes. Douglas placed his foot on the briefcase beneath his seat and yawned. No good trying to fall asleep now. He leaned forward and took the airline magazine from the seat pocket. VIVA LAS VEGAS! was written across the front, underneath which a showgirl in white peacock feathers danced. Douglas skimmed the articles. There were the exotic fish of Afghanistan, the wild nightlife of Baghdad, the lively markets of Lebanon. To have a job transporting souls to those countries—now *there* was the courier job to have. Better yet was securing an upper management job engineering the transmission of souls into crystals. That meant knowing how to scan souls for undesirable elements, download pro-government sentiment, and replace unwanted memories with product loyalty. You needed an incarnation of training to secure a job like that. All the same, perhaps that was the way to go. Douglas's fingers paused mid-turn. A photo on the VIVA LAS VEGAS! page made his abdomen grow cold.

Between the white lights of Las Vegas's unfinished Tower of Babel Casino stood the world famous Luxor. The white pyramid rose like a phantom memory. A thought flashed across Douglas's mind like an instant blink. *You've forgotten what you came to do.* Douglas had a sudden feeling of despair, and the accompanying awful sensation of an unreachable memory. For God's sake, flip the page. But he couldn't, and as he looked at the pyramid rising from the neon-lit metropolis, a thick coil of heat unraveled in his belly. He put his hands against his abdomen to calm the feeling, but as his palms touched his stomach, a memory flashed clear as a high-definition image. He was standing on the ridge of a temple.

Far below, a skinny white man stood yelling through a bull-horn. *We've Got You Surrounded!* The woman grabbed his hand. "Remember me," she said.

Douglas pulled his hands away from his belly as though they'd been burned. For the love of God, what was going on? Something was very wrong with him. He needed to log back on and take a couple Percodextrins and a Metabutronol, but that wouldn't be possible until they landed. A drink then, he thought. Indeed. A drink, and some food, and then, if they were showing a movie, he'd pay the money and keep himself entertained for the rest of the flight. The plane was rolling down the runway, picking up speed. The tip of the plane tilted up, a perfect diagonal against the earth, as precise as the ridge of a pyramid. His finger was still holding the page open, the Luxor staring back at him. Outside, the sun blazed white, its belly submerged in the clouds like a God and, though he knew he shouldn't, Douglas stared at the sun as if in deep meditation.

✹

THE HUMMER WAS waiting for Douglas at the rental place. The Apex attendant downloaded the keys into Douglas's system and Douglas set the coordinates for Colfax. As the Hummer navigated Denver's ribbon of highway, Douglas relaxed in his seat. The Percodextrin and Metabutronol had helped him feel calmer and, after taking the second Alertin, Douglas felt like himself again. The billboards along the free-

way blinked white against the night sky. KEEBLER FROZIE
MOCHA TREATS—SIMPLY FANTA*SS*TIC! a sign broadcast, beneath
which a woman's ass pushed suggestively toward the passing car.

When the Hummer parallel parked on Colfax, Douglas
sent an instant blink to Phillip Monto. He made sure the
briefcase was hidden beneath the seat, then got out of his car
and activated the security alarm. Halfway down the block,
the neon lights of two buttocks flashed into the night. Beneath the sign was a skinny white man in a suit. The man
raised his hand into the air. "Hey there!" Monto's words
echoed across the concrete. Douglas's belly went cold. The
man was waving a bullhorn. *Hey there! We've got you surrounded!* The pale neon lights of the buttocks made Monto's
features appear distorted and grotesque, his grinning teeth
gleaming.

"You made it, chief!" Monto said, lowering his hand,
which held a smoldering cigarette. He pulled his other hand
from his pocket and shook Douglas's. "Flight go all right?"

Douglas released Monto's grip and wiped his brow.
"Besides five-hour delays, bad food, and being an overall
pain in the ass, not bad."

Monto blinked a couple times. "Oh yeah, yeah. Well, what
can you expect? Air travel: complete hell. Well, listen, I hope
I'm not being presumptuous here, but I heard you were an
ass man."

"Who isn't?" Douglas said.

"Dalai Lama, that's fucking who! Bunch of bullshit is what I say; I bet he's in his cave right now wishing he had some ass!" He gave Douglas another skeletal grin.

"Probably got all the Buddhist ass he needs," Douglas said.

"Even so, the guy's missing out." Monto gestured with his cigarette toward the doors of Rocky Mounds. "Best Live-Ass club in Denver. They got all types in there. White, African, Asian. Come on, let's get you a drink." And though Douglas had the urge to retreat to the vault of his Hummer, he followed Monto through the doors.

The dim lights of the club cast shadows on the men sitting at the tables. Waitresses flittered through the room like ghosts, their short white skirts pulled up high to reveal a glimpse of their buttocks. Monto took a table near the stage. "What can I get you?" he asked.

"Mojito, if they've got it. Otherwise I'll take—"

"Hey, you're in the best club in Denver, they've got it."

"Here, let me send you some credits." Douglas pulled up his accounts page.

"Don't even try," Monto winked. "I'm blocking any credit downloads from you tonight. Soul Co.'s treating. Couriers have to enjoy some benefits."

Douglas sat back in his chair. Lit by stage lights, three women, one African, one white, one Asian, bounced their asses in time with a DJ playing drum and bass. Over the music, the words *Ass, Ass, Ass* pounded. The asses were thick, rich, and voluptuous, like silky mountains of—and there it was again, an infuriating unreachable tingle between his legs. Douglas's belly began to spasm. He instinctively placed his hands on his stomach to calm himself. As his palms touched his abdomen a vision flashed in his mind. He was in bed with the woman; she was kissing his face, his neck, his lips; a candle flickered against the wall; the shadow of a moth flittered against the flame, circling and circling before catching fire.

"What did I tell you? Not bad, huh?" Monto said as the waitress brought their drinks.

"What?" Douglas asked. His body was covered in a thin film of sweat. He removed his hands from his belly. "Oh yeah. That white ass is top notch."

"I'm an Asian guy myself. Man, just look at those pillows. Yeah, baby! Make that ass clap!" He lifted his glass toward Douglas. "Hey, here's to Soul Co.!"

"To Soul Co.," Douglas responded, and the men clinked.

"So, you've got some pretty heavy luggage with you?"

"Fifty-seven souls."

Monto let out a whistle. "Damn. You *must* be good. Boss said to me, you take this guy out, show him a good time—he works for the big guy. So, I had it all set up for us tonight, wine and dine on the budget. On the budget! Shame your flight was delayed, they've got a great steakhouse out here. Porterhouse rounds big as that African ass up there. Soft as it, too! Hey, Soul Co. knows how to make it happen. Right? Right!" Monto took a sip of his drink. "But tell me something, you ever seen any Buddhist ass?"

"Wouldn't want to."

"Nah, me neither, but you have to wonder what those asses look like."

Douglas took a sip of his drink. He turned his eyes to the stage. The girls had their hands on their knees and were thrusting their asses toward him. Douglas's stomach convulsed. He needed to get some cold water on his face.

"Where's the bathroom?"

"Right side of the bar." Monto nodded his bony chin toward the back of the club.

Douglas's legs felt hollow as he rose. He navigated through the murky light, waitresses flittering past like spirits, the music throbbing in his temples. He slammed against the bathroom door and entered the white-tiled glow of the men's room.

He chose a urinal, unzipped his pants, and pulled out his penis. It hung limply as a thin stream trickled from its tip. His belly was beginning to feel better, and he let out a breath of relief and looked up. There, among the scribbled graffiti, was a crude drawing of a pyramid with an eye at its center. Douglas's belly went cold. He put his hand against the wall to keep himself from falling over. *In God We Trust.* The memory jangled through his mind.

That'll be three-twenty five, due back next Saturday.

They'd rented a movie. She'd suggested a comedy, and

he'd put the pyramids down one after another on the counter beneath the fluorescents. The light of the awning as they exited the store had lit her face so beautifully, and the color of the awning had been . . . not white . . . but . . . Blockbuster. That was her name! She was Blockbuster! It'd been cold. There was snow falling. There was a couch. He'd paid with pyramids, and they'd never finished the movie. She'd pressed against him and said, "I'm sleepy." And the moth had flown into the candle as she held the pyramid to the light.

But, no, that was all wrong. It wasn't after a video. The video rental had happened in a previous incarnation. She'd held a dollar bill in the light of the candle so he could look at it, their daughter asleep in the adjacent room, and she'd said, "This is to help you remember."

"What is it?"

"We used these in our last lifetime. When you infiltrate Soul Co. they're going to remove your memories of the revolution. You have to work on recalling your past incarnations like we've been doing. Remember this pyramid," she said. "The resistance will paint this symbol everywhere to help you remember. We'll build the temple for the arrival of the Dalai Lama. If they destroy us before we finish, it's up to you to find us again."

"I'll remember," he'd promised. "It might take incarnations, but I'll work my way in. I'll destroy Soul Co. from the top down." But his voice had been shaking, as though he could hear the tanks that would soon be rolling toward them.

Then the moth flew into the candle, shocking them both, and it rose like some ancient Sun God, flames shooting from its wings as it kicked its legs into empty air. She rolled atop him and kissed him. No, she took him by the hand and they ran down the temple steps, sand beneath his feet. "We haven't made it this time!" Pushing further, his hands around her naked body, her hands on his stomach, his hands around another stone, scooping up mortar, sun blazing hot, sweating, lay down the stone, slide the mortar, push it down, holding on to her as she placed both hands against his chest and rocked against him, push, slide, rise, push, slide, rise, right hand holding troth, scooping mortar, brick down, push, slide, rise, push, slide, rise, candle bursting into brilliant light against her belly, flame shooting through the crown of her head, down through her heart, down though her abdomen, and into him in a flash of white light.

And now, penis drained, Douglas realized in horror that his limp appendage, lifeless for incarnations, was beginning to rise. It moved like a serpent charmed by the pulsing in his pelvis, and stretched its neck toward the toilet mint of the urinal, ready to devour it. *Ass, Ass, Ass.* The music pounded as the door to the men's room slammed open.

"God! I just love those asses!" a man in jeans and a white T-shirt said as he sidled up next to Douglas. Douglas looked down at his penis. It was still stretching toward the porcelain. Sweat dripping down his neck, he stuffed his penis into his pants and zipped his fly. "Ain't those the best asses in the Rockies?" the man yelled.

"I don't know," Douglas said, stumbling toward the door.

He careened into the club. The women were on the stage, putting their hands on their knees, pushing their asses toward him. Phillip Monto, in his thin white suit, turned to face him. As he did, the lights hit his face, and Monto's skull opened into a wide grin. *This is Sergeant Monto, we've got you surrounded!*

"Thought you got lost!" Monto said.

Douglas looked down at himself. His pants were still bulging abnormally. He put his hand in his pocket and held his penis against his leg. "I think I'm going to call it a night," he said. "I'm bushed."

"You're kidding me, it's only eleven! Hell, bars don't close here till three. Come on, Doug. On the budget! You want to go somewhere else? There's a place with straight Latina ass. That your style? You a Latina kind of guy?"

"It's not that." Douglas braced himself against the table. "I've just had an exhausting day."

"I can't lie, you look bad. You need some Wellamutrin? I'll send you as many as you need."

"No, really, I'm fine. I just need to get some sleep."

"Well, hell, man, I'm sorry to see you go. Night was just getting started!" Monto's tone was meant as jovial, but Douglas saw the look of distrust behind his eyes. Monto was blinking off an eyemail. *Something wrong with this carrier.* Douglas could see the bones through the skin as Monto extended his hand. He grasped it and shook, the bones rattling beneath his grip.

Douglas clambered away from the table. He pushed past the bouncers and stumbled through the doors of the entrance out beneath the neon lights of the buttocks, taking deep gulps of air. Breathe, Douglas, breathe. There's something wrong with you. Make a technician appointment the moment you get back to Manhattan. Breathe.

He made his way back to the rental car, swiped his wrist across the door handle, got in, and shut the door. Thank God he was back in his Hummer. He took a couple of deep breaths and looked down at his pants. They looked as flat as ever. Douglas wiped the sweat from his forehead. A little Innercourse on the ride to the hotel would relax him. It was already 1:00 A.M. in New York, but it might not be too late to blink K-5478. Yes, some Innercourse, a couple of Seconal, a good night's rest, and he'd be okay. But then, at the top right of his screen, a white rag caught his attention. Douglas had time to utter a short yelp before the cloth covered his mouth; then his eyelids closed with the sigh of a computer shutting down.

❋

ALONG THE RED Mountain Pass of Colorado stands an abandoned gas station. Its pumps are red with rust, the old computer pads for ATM cards smashed. The Mini Mart, once stocked with Keebler snacks, cola, and other goods for the Mesa Verde–bound traveler, is empty. The windows of the station are broken. Dust has sifted in through the jagged glass for centuries. It has piled like snow on the counter where gas attendants once stood, and buried the toppled Doritos racks, whose metal ribs rise from the dirt like the bones of dinosaurs. Sediment has drifted into tall spires along the corners of the room. In this desolate location, among the forgotten blisters of National Parks, too costly to develop, too pointless to destroy, a green scarab beetle of a car comes to rest. Four yellow hoods step from the Toyota hatchback. They pull a man from the backseat.

Around the side of the building are two doors with white lettering. MEN. WOMEN. The tallest individual produces a key and opens the Women's door. Inside, a circular stone staircase leads down. They carry the body into the belly of a cavern, where the air is damp and the walls are knotted with pine roots. The yellow hoods drag the man through an archway into the main chamber. One of the hoods walks along the perimeter of the room, and from his hand springs the egg-shaped flame of a lighter. He brings the flame down and lights wick after wick.

A steel hospital gurney rests in the center, reflecting the candles as though lined with a dozen fiery eyes. Upon a cold tray lie a scalpel, scissors, needles and thread, and a basin of water. The scissors are lifted and placed by the man's throat. Their sharpened edges slice through his collar, shearing his shirt from his torso. Then his pants and boxers are sliced open. He is flipped onto his stomach.

"Are we ready?" a female hood asks. The assembled group nods. She picks up the scalpel and places the cold blade against the skin of the man's spine. The assembled group begins to chant. *Om mani padme hum, om mani padme hum.* As the blade splits the flesh, the man's eyes open, Innervision screens suddenly alive. Send off an eyemail! Send off an eyemail! Broadcast your location!

A white rag is placed over the man's nose and mouth, his pupils turning a dull gray as Innervision goes blank. The tall one leans down, her yellow hood close to the man's ear. "Don't be afraid," she whispers. "You're being liberated."

※

THE FIRST THING Douglas noticed when he opened his eyes was that the sky had broken. Thick liquid oozed from clouds and covered the horizon. There were no words for the substance that plastered the sky, and the sight hurt Douglas's naked retinas.

"You're finally awake," a woman said. She came over and sat on the cot. "How do you feel?" She picked up a washcloth from a basin and dabbed his eyes with cool water. He turned his head to look at her, and saw yet another frightening sight. The thick liquid that oozed from the clouds had seeped into her features, tinting her face not white, nor black, nor gray.

He opened his mouth to speak but all that came out was a moan.

"Shhh," the woman said, putting her hands on his abdomen. "You don't have to be afraid. You're seeing colors. It's a beautiful experience."

The sound of the woman's voice and her hands on his belly brought clarity and, with it, panic. Fragments of memories circled like burning moths: the neon buttocks of Rocky Mounds, his head banging against the glass of a car window, trying to log on to Innernet before the yellow hoods realized he was awake, watching the scalpel lowered toward his eye.

Behind the woman, a gruesome edifice split the sky. They were in a massive open cavern. Clay buildings with hollow windows rose from the ground like a city of sand. The rock faces bled color. Then, with horror, Douglas saw the framed photo of the Dalai Lama hanging on the wall. In that moment, as Douglas lay on a cot in Mesa Verde, his greatest fear was confirmed: he was being held hostage by Buddhist terrorists. He blinked in rapid succession, trying to pull up Innervision to send off a distress signal. His eyelids closed and opened. There was no small clock at the bottom of his vision, no EyeDate iconography along his left periphery.

"It's gone," the woman said. Douglas looked at her and tried to blink again. Nothing. Just her face, the color of the cliff walls, and her eyes, the color of the sky, as though her retinas were holes through which he could see the world. Her eyelids, however, were trembling. "Do you remember who I am?" she asked.

Perhaps if he answered right, told her what she wanted to hear, they wouldn't execute him. Douglas focused on her face, the age lines around her mouth and eyes, the gray speckled through her hair. The colors brought out the freckles spread across her cheeks. Douglas had remembered her name once, back at Rocky Mounds. The bathroom, the graffiti on the wall, she had wanted to rent a comedy, it was snowing. "Blockbuster!" he said. "I remember you. Your name's Blockbuster! Listen, Blockbuster, I just want to go home. Please. I can give you whatever you want."

She brought her hand to her face and wiped her tears. She smiled. "It's okay," she said. "I should've expected you wouldn't recognize me; I don't look the same anymore. Natural reincarnation does that to you. You'll remember; it'll take some time." She got up from the cot. "I'll make you a cup of tea."

Against the far wall stood a clay hearth with a fire smoldering. Atop it lay a piece of sheet metal. The woman took a teakettle from the floor and placed it onto the makeshift stove. "This is where we live now," she said. "It's the only place they haven't found us. I've saved your journals to help you remember," she nodded toward the side of the cot where a stack of books was piled, their pages yellow, the covers dirty with dust. "We've been rebuilding the temple," she added. "It's nearly finished."

The teakettle was whistling. The woman raised the

steaming pot from the stove and lowered it toward the two clay mugs. She poured the boiling water, placed the teapot onto the ground, and carried the cups toward Douglas.

"It's chamomile," she said, setting the mug by the side of his cot. "It used to be your favorite." The steam wafted up, the smell familiar, earthy and sweet. "Louis, I know you're frightened." The name wiggled through Douglas's mind like a lost memory. "It's okay, you're safe now. You tried the best you could. We've already smashed the crystals you brought. Their souls have returned to the natural cycle of reincarnation." She placed her hands against his belly, the feeling of her palms familiar against his skin.

"Please, Blockbuster," Douglas begged, "what do you want from me?"

"Nothing," she said. Lowering her face against his, she pressed her lips upon his eyelids. In the darkness of his logged-off mind, she whispered, "I'm just glad you're home."

ROCKET NIGHT

IT WAS ROCKET Night at our daughter's elementary school, the night when parents, students, and administrators gather to place the least-liked child in a rocket and shoot him into the stars. Last year we placed Laura Jackson into the capsule, a short, squat girl known for the limp dresses that hung crookedly on her body. The previous year we'd sent off a boy from India whose name none of us could remember.

Rocket Night falls in late October when the earth is covered by leaves. Our children have begun to lay out their Halloween costumes, and their sweaters are heavy with the scent of autumn. It's late enough into the school year for us to get a sense of the best children to send off. Alliances are made early at Rose Hill. Our children gather in the mornings to share their secrets on the playground, while the other children—those with stars and galaxies in their futures—can be seen at the edges of the field, playing alone with sticks or staring into mud puddles at drowned worms.

In the school gymnasium, we mingle in the warm glow of lacquered floors, surrounded by wooden bleachers and parallel bars, talking about soccer games, math homework, and the difficulty of finding time for errands with our children's busy schedules. Our kids run the perimeter, some playing tag, others collecting in clusters of boys around the fifth-graders with portable game consoles, the girls across the room in their own clusters. Susan Beech brought her famous home-baked cupcakes, the Stowes brought Hawaiian Punch, and we brought plastic cups and cocktail napkins and placed them on the table among the baked goods and apple slices.

The boy to be sent off, I believe his name was Daniel, stood near his parents, holding his mother's skirt, looking unkempt. One could immediately see the reason he'd been chosen. The mildewed scent of thrift stores clung to his corduroys, and his collar sat askew, revealing the small white undershirt beneath. His brown slacks were held up by an oversize belt, the end of which flopped lazily from his side. The boy, our daughter told us, brought stubby pencils to school whose chewed-up ends got stuck in sharpeners. He had the habit of picking his nose and wiping it on his pants. His lunches were nothing more than stale crackers and a warm box of chocolate milk. There was a smear of cupcake frosting on the corner of his mouth, and upon seeing this detail, we knew our children had chosen well. He was the sort of child who makes one proud of one's own children, and we looked over to our daughter, who was holding court with a devil's square, tightening then spreading her small fingers within the folded paper while counting out the letters O-R-A-N-G-E.

At eight o'clock the principal took the stage beneath the basketball hoop, a whine from the microphone as he adjusted it. He turned to us with open arms and welcomed parents and students to another year at Rose Hill. He thanked Susan for her cupcakes, and all of us for our contributions to the evening's festivities. Then, forgetting the boy's name, he turned to the family and said, "We hope your child's journey into space will be a joyful one." We all applauded. His parents applauded less than others, looking a bit pale, but parents of the chosen often seem pale. They are the sort of people who come to soccer games and sit alone in the stands, a gloomy sadness hanging over them, whose cars make the most noise when they pull into our school's parking lot, and whose faces, within the automobile's dark interiors, remind us of a sorrow none of us wish to share.

His speech delivered, the principal invited us to join him on the playground where the capsule sat, cockpit open, its silver sides illuminated by the glow from the launch tower. It's a truth that the child to be sent into space grows reticent upon seeing the glowing tower and the gaping, casketlike rocket. We saw the small boy cling to his mother, unwilling to leave her side, and so we let our children loose. I watched my daughter pry the boy's fingers from his mother's leg as two larger fifth-graders seized his waist and dragged him away. The nurse, a kindly woman, helped to subdue the parents.

She took the mother aside and whispered to her while the gym coach placed a meaty hand on the father's shoulder and assured him that the capsule was stocked with water and food tablets, plenty to last the boy a long time into the future. To be honest, it's a mystery how long such supplies last. It's a small compartment within that capsule and we are all aware funding was cut to our district earlier this year, but still we assured them there was nothing to fear. The boy, if hungry for company, had a small microphone inside the shell, which would allow him to speak to himself about his journey, his thoughts, and the mysteries of the universe.

The boy was strapped into the capsule, his hands secured, and he looked out at us. He spoke then, for the first and only time that night. He asked if he might have one of his pencils with him; it was in his pencil box, he said, the one with a brown bear eraser. The principal assured him that he wouldn't need it in outer space, and the custodian noted that the request was moot; the boy's desk had been emptied earlier that day. So, they closed the cover. All we could see was the smudge of the boy's face pressed against the porthole.

When the rocket blasted off, it made us all take an involuntary step backward, the light of the flames illuminating the wonder upon our children's faces. The capsule rose from the playground, leaving behind our swing sets and jungle gym, rising higher, until it was a sparkling marble in the night sky, and then, finally, gone. We sighed with awe, some applauded, and then we made our rounds, wishing one another goodnight, arranging play dates, and returning to our cars. Those of us on the PTO remained to put the gymnasium back in order for next morning. And the boy faded from our thoughts, replaced by the lateness of the evening and the pressure of delayed bedtime schedules. I had all but forgotten about the child by the time I laid our sleeping daughter on her bed. And yet, when I took out the recycling that night, I paused beneath the streetlamps of our cul-de-sac and thought of all the children high above. I imagined them drifting alone up there, speaking into their microphones, reporting to themselves about the depths of the unknown.

OPENNESS

BEFORE I DECIDED to finally give up on New York, I subbed classes at a junior high in Brooklyn. A sixth-grade math teacher suffering from downloading anxiety was out for the year, and jobs being what they were, I took any opportunity I could. Subbing math was hardly my dream job; I had a degree in visual art, for which I'd be in debt for the rest of my life. All I had to show for it was my senior collection, a series of paintings of abandoned playgrounds, stored in a U-Pack shed in Ohio. There was a time when I'd imagined I'd become famous, give guest lectures at colleges, and have retrospectives at MOMA. Instead, I found myself standing in front of a class of apathetic tweens, trying to teach them how to do long division without accessing their browsers. I handed out pen and paper, so that for once in their lives they'd have a tactile experience, and watched as they texted, their eyes glazed from blinking off message after message. They spent most of the class killing vampires and orcs inside their heads and humoring me by lazily filling out my photocopies.

The city overwhelmed me. Every day I'd walk by hundreds of strangers, compete for space in crowded coffee shops, and stand shoulder to shoulder on packed subway cars. I'd scan profiles, learning that the woman waiting for the N enjoyed thrash-hop, and the barista at my local coffee shop loved salted caramel. I'd had a couple fleeting relationships, but mostly I'd spend weekends going to bars and sleeping with people who knew little more than my username. It all made me want to turn off my layers, go back to the old days, and stay disconnected. But you do that and you become another old guy buried in an e-reader, complaining about how no one sends emails anymore.

So, I stayed open, shared the most superficial info of my outer layer with the world, and filtered through everyone I passed, hoping to find some connection. Here was citycat5, jersygirl13, m3love. And then, one morning, there was Katie, sitting across from me on the N. She was lakegirl03, and her hair fell from under her knit cap. The only other info I could access was her hometown and that she was single.

"Hi," I winked, and when I realized she had her tunes on, I sent off an invite. She raised her eyes.

"Hi," she winked back.

"You're from Maine? I'm planning a trip there this summer. Any suggestions?"

She leaned forward, and warmth spread across my chest

from being allowed into her second layer. "I'm Katie," she winked. "You should visit Bar Harbor, I grew up there." She gave me access to an image of a lake house with tall silvery pines rising high above the shingled roof. "Wish I could help more, but this is my stop." As she stood waiting for the doors to open, I winked a last message. *Can I invite you for a drink?* The train hissed, the doors opened, and she looked back at me and smiled before disappearing into the mass of early morning commuters. It was as the train sped toward work that her contact info appeared in my mind, along with a photo of her swimming in a lake at dusk.

✵

IT TURNED OUT that Katie had been in the city for a couple years before she'd found a steady job. She taught senior citizens how to successfully navigate their layers. She'd helped a retired doctor upload images of his grandchildren so strangers could congratulate him, and assisted a ninety-three-year-old widow in sharing her mourning with the world. Her main challenge, she said, was getting older folks to understand the value of their layers.

"Every class they ask me why we can't just talk instead," she shared as we lay in bed. Though Katie and I occasionally spoke, it was always accompanied by layers. It was tiring to labor through the sentences needed to explain how you ran into a friend—much easier to share the memory, the friend's name and photo appearing organically.

"At least they still want to speak. My class won't even say hello."

"You remember what it was like before?" she asked. I tried to think back to high school, but it was fuzzy. I was sure we used to talk more, but it seemed like we doled out personal details in hushed tones.

"Not really," I said. "Do you?"

"Sure. My family's cabin is completely out of range. Whenever I go back we can only talk."

"What's *that* like?"

She shared a photo of walking in the woods with her father, the earth covered in snow, and I felt the sharp edge of jealousy. Back where I grew up, there hadn't been any pristine forests to walk through, just abandoned mini-marts, a highway, and trucks heading past our town, which was more a pit stop than a community. The only woods were behind the high school, a small dangerous place where older kids might drag you if you didn't run fast enough. And my parents sure didn't talk. My mother was a clinical depressive who'd spent my childhood either behind the closed door of her bedroom or at the kitchen table, doing crossword puzzles and telling me to be quiet whenever I asked her something. My father had hit me so hard that twice I'd blacked out. My history wasn't the kind of thing I wanted to unlock for anyone, and since leaving Ohio I'd done my best to bury those memories within my layers.

So, I spent our first months sharing little of myself. Katie showed me the memories of her best friends and family while I showed her the mundane details of substitute teaching and my favorite bands. I knew Katie could feel the contours of my hidden memories, like stones beneath a bedsheet, but for a while she let me keep the private pain of my unlocked layers.

※

THAT SUMMER, KATIE invited me to spend the weekend with her dad at their cabin. We rented a car and drove up the coast to Maine. We listened to our favorite songs, made pit stops, and finally left I-95 for the local roads. It was late in the afternoon, our car completely shaded by the pines, when our reception started getting spotty. I could feel my connection with Katie going in and out.

"Guess we might as well log off," Katie said. She closed her eyes for a moment, and all of a sudden I felt a chasm open between us. There was a woman sitting next to me whom I had no access to. "It's okay, babe," she said, and reached out for my hand. "I'm still me." I pressed my palm to hers, closed my eyes, and logged off, too.

Her father, Ben, was a big man who wore a puffy green vest that made him appear even larger. "And you're Andy," he said, burying my hand in his. "Let me get those bags for you." He hefted both our suitcases from the trunk, leaving me feeling useless. I followed him into the house, experiencing the quiet Katie had told me about. There were no messages coming from anyone, no buzz-posts to read, just the three of us in the cabin and the hum of an ancient refrigerator.

The last time a girlfriend had introduced me to her parents we'd sat at Applebee's making small talk from outer layer info, but with Ben, there were no layers to access. All I knew were the details Katie had shared with me. I knew that her mom had died when she was fourteen, and that her father had spent a year at the cabin grieving, but that didn't seem like anything to bring up. So, I stood there, looking out the living room window, trying to remember how people used to talk back in the days when we knew nothing about each other.

"Katie says you've never been to Maine."

"I haven't," I said, the words feeling strange against my tongue.

He walked over to the living room window. The afternoon sun shimmered on the pond, making it look silvery and alive, and the sky was wide and blue, pierced only by the spires of red pines. "Beautiful, isn't it?"

"Yeah," I said. The fridge hummed and from the other room I could hear Katie opening drawers and unpacking. I wasn't sure what else to add. I remembered a detail she had unlocked for me on one of our early dates. "I heard you've caught a lot of fish out there."

"You like fishing?" he asked, placing his hand on my shoulder. "Here, I'll show you something."

Ben retrieved an old tablet from the closet and showed

me photos on the screen. There he was with Katie and a string of fish; him scaling a trout in the kitchen sink. We scrolled through the two-dimensional images one by one as people did when I was a kid. Katie came to my rescue. "Come on, I want to show you the lake," she said. "Dad can wow you with his antique technology later."

"One day you'll be happy I kept this," he said. "Katie's baby photos are all on here." He shut down the device and put it back in its case. "Have fun out there. Dinner will be ready in an hour."

Outside, Katie led me on the trails I'd only ever seen in her layers. Here was the gnarled cedar that she'd built a fort beneath, and over there were the rocks she'd chipped mica flakes from in second grade. We climbed down the banks of the trail, holding on to roots that jutted from the earth, and arrived on a stretch of sand speckled with empty clam shells, mussels, and snails that clung to the wet stones. Far down the beach, a rock outcropping rose from the water. A single heron stood on a peak that broke the shoreline.

There was something beautiful about sharing things in the old way—the two of us walking by the shore, the smell of the pine sap, the summer air cooling the late afternoon—and for the first time in years, I wished I had a sketch pad with me. As Katie spoke, her hands moved in ways I hadn't seen people do since childhood, gesturing toward the lake or me when she got excited. I tried to focus on each sentence, sensing my brain's inability to turn her words into pictures.

She was talking about the cabin in autumn, logs burning in the fireplace, the smell of smoke, leaves crunching underfoot.

"Are you even listening?" she asked when I didn't respond.

"Sorry," I said. "I'm trying to. It's just that without the *ding* it's hard to know when you're sending . . . I mean *saying* something. . . ." I stopped talking, hating the clunkiness of words, and took a deep breath. "I guess I'm just rusty."

Katie softened. "I know. Sometimes when I'm in the city, I can't remember what it looks like up here without accessing my photos. It's kinda messed up, isn't it?"

"Yeah," I agreed, "I guess it is." The heron hunched down and then lifted off, its wide wings flapping as it headed across the lake, away from us.

❈

THAT NIGHT HER father fried up the perch he'd caught earlier that day. The herbs and butter filled the small cabin with their scent, and we drank the wine we'd brought. After dinner, Ben brought out a blue cardboard box, and the three of us sat in the living room and played an actual game. I hadn't seen one in over a decade.

"You don't know how to play Boggle?" Katie asked, surprised. The point, she explained, was to make words from the lettered dice and to write them down with pen and paper without accessing other players' thoughts. I sat there trying to figure out what Katie was feeling as she covered her paper with her hand.

"What do you think?" Katie asked after the first round.

"It's fun," I admitted.

"You bet it is," Ben said, and made the dice rattle again.

When Katie and I were in bed, I listened to the crickets outside the screened windows. It'd been a long time since I'd heard the drone of them, each one singing within the chorus.

"So, what do you think of it here?"

"It's beautiful. But I can't imagine growing up without connection."

"You don't like the feeling?"

"Not really," I said. Being offline reminded me of my life back home before layers existed, when I'd lived with my parents in Ohio, a miserable time that technology had helped to bury. "Do you?"

"Totally. I could live like this forever." I looked at her in the dark and tried to scan her eyes, but it was just her looking back at me, familiar yet completely different. "What about my dad?"

"I like him," I said, though it was only part of the truth. I was really thinking how different he was from my own father. We never sat and ate dinner together or played board games. I'd heat up frozen pizza and eat it in the kitchen while Dad would lie on the couch watching whatever game was on.

Eventually, he'd get up, clink the bottles into the bin, and that was the sign to shut off the TV. Thinking about it made me feel like Katie and her father were playing a joke on me. There was no way people actually lived like this—without yelling, without fighting.

I felt the warmth of Katie's hand against my chest. "What's the matter?"

"Nothing."

"You can tell me," she said. *"I love you."*

It was the first time she'd actually said the words. At home it was just something we knew. We understood it from the moments we'd stand brushing our teeth together and the feeling would flash through her layers. And sometimes, late at night, right before we'd both fall asleep, we'd reach out and touch each other's hands and feel it.

"I love you, too," I managed to get out, and the weight of the words made something shift inside me. I felt the sentences forming in my head, the words lining up as though waiting to be released. Without my layers, there was nothing to keep them from spilling out. "Katie," I said into the darkness. "I want to tell you about my family."

She put her arms around me. "Okay."

And there, in the cabin, feeling Katie's body against mine, I began to speak. I didn't stop myself, but leaned into my voice and the comfort of hearing my words disappearing into the air with only Katie and the crickets as witnesses.

✺

IT WAS THAT night in the cabin that helped us grow closer. Shortly after we returned, I unlocked more layers for her and showed her the pictures of my father and mother—the few I'd kept. There was my high school graduation: my mother's sunken eyes staring at the camera, my father with his hands in his pockets, and me in between, none of us happy. I showed her the dirty vinyl-sided house and the denuded lawn, blasted by cold winters and the perpetual dripping oil from my father's truck. And she showed me her own hidden layers: her mother's funeral in a small church in Maine, her father escaping to the cabin afterward, learning to cook dinner for herself. Having unlocked the bad memories, I also uncovered the few good ones I'd hidden: a snowy day, my father, in a moment of tenderness, pulling me on a sled through the town; my mother emerging from her room shortly before she died to give me a hug as I left for school.

Feeling the closeness that sharing our layers brought, Katie suggested we give total openness a shot. It meant offering our most painful wounds as a gift to one another, a testament that there was no corner of the soul so ugly as to remain unshared. It'd become increasingly common to see the couples in Brooklyn, a simple *O* tattooed around their fingers announcing the radical honesty of their relationship to the world. They went to Open House parties, held in abandoned meatpacking plants, where partiers let down all their layers and displayed the infinite gradations of pain and joy to strangers while DJs played breaknoise directly into their heads. I resented the couples, imagining them to be suburban hipsters who'd grown up with loving parents, regular allowances, and easy histories to share.

Total openness seemed premature, I told Katie, not just for us but for everyone. Our culture was still figuring out the technology. A decade after linking in, I'd find drinking episodes that had migrated to my work layer or, worse yet, porn clips that I had to flush back down into the darkness of my hidden layers.

"I'm not going to judge you," she promised as we lay in bed. She put her leg over mine. "You do realize how hot it'll be to know each other's fantasies, right?" There were dozens of buzz-posts about it—the benefits of total intimacy, how there were no more fumbling mistakes, no guessing, just a personal database of kinks that could be accessed by your partner.

"What about the darker layers?"

"We need to uncover those, too," Katie said. "That's what love is: seeing all the horrible stuff and still loving each other."

I thought I understood it then, and though my heart was in my throat, my terror so palpable that my body had gone cold, I was willing to believe that total openness wasn't the opposite of safety but the only true guarantee of finding it. So late that summer evening, Katie and I sat on the bed, gazing into one another's eyes, and we gave each other total access.

I'VE SPENT A lot of time thinking about what went wrong, whether total openness was to blame or not. Some days I think it was, that there's no way to share the totality of yourself and still be loved, that secrets are the glue that holds relationships together. Other times, I think Katie and I weren't meant to be a couple for the long haul; total openness just helped us find the end more quickly. Maybe it was nothing more than the limits of the software. We were the first generation to grow up with layers, a group of kids who'd produced thousands of tutorials on blocking unwanted users but not a single one on empathy.

There were certainly good things that came from openness. Like how, after finding my paintings, Katie surprised me with a sketch pad and a set of drawing pencils. Or the nights when I'd come home from a frustrating day of substitute teaching and she'd have accessed my mood long before I saw her. She'd lay me down on the bed and give me a massage without us even winking one another. But all too often, it was the things we didn't need to share that pierced our love: sexual histories that left Katie stewing for weeks; fleeting attractions to waiters and waitresses when we'd go out to dinner; momentary annoyances that would have been best left unshared. Letting someone into every secret gave access to our dark corners, and rather than feeling sympathy for each other's failings, we blamed each other for nearsightedness, and soon layers of resentment were dredged up. There was a night at the bar when I watched Katie struggling to speak loudly enough for the bartender to hear, and I suddenly realized his face resembled the schoolyard bully of her childhood. "You have to get over that already," I blinked angrily. Soon after, while watching a film I wasn't enjoying, she tapped into layers I hadn't yet registered. "He's just a fictional character, not your father."

And then there was the final New Year's Eve party at her friend's place out in Bay Ridge. The party was Y2K-themed, and guests were expected to actually speak to one another. A bunch of partygoers were sporting Bluetooth headsets into which they yelled loudly. We listened to Jamiroquai on a boom box and watched Teletubbies on a salvaged flat-screen. Katie was enjoying herself. She danced to the songs and barely winked anyone, happy to be talking again. I tried to be sociable, but I was shut down, giving access only to my most superficial layers as everyone got drunk and sloppy with theirs.

We stood talking to a guy wearing an ironic trucker's cap as he pretended we were in 1999. "So, you think the computers are going to blow up at midnight?" he asked us.

Katie laughed.

"No," I said.

"Come on," Katie blinked. *"Loosen up."*

"I'm not into the kitsch," I blinked back.

"Mostly I'm just excited about faxing things," the guy in the trucker's cap joked, and Katie laughed again.

"You know faxing was the early nineties, right?" I said, and then blinked to Katie, *"Are you flirting with this guy?"*

"All I'm saying is check out this Bluetooth. Can you believe folks wore these?"

"I know, that's crazy," Katie said. *"No, I'm not flirting. I'm talking. How about you try it for a change?"*

"I told you, I don't like talking."

"Great, so you're never going to want to talk, then?"

"Did you guys make any New Year's resolutions?" the guy asked us.

"Yeah," Katie said, looking at me, "to talk more." In her annoyance an image from a deeper layer flashed into clear resolution. It was a glimpse of a future she'd imagined for herself, and I saw us canoeing in Maine, singing songs with our kids. Even though we'd discussed how I never wanted children, there they were, and while I hadn't sung aloud since grade school, there was a projection of me singing. Only then did I see the other incongruities. My eyes were blue not brown, my voice buoyant, my physique way more buff than I ever planned to become. And though I shared similarities with the man in the canoe, as if Katie had tried to fit me into his mold, the differences were clear. There in the canoe, was the family Katie wanted, and the man with her wasn't me.

"What the fuck?" I said aloud.

"It's just a question," the guy said. "If it's personal, you don't have to share. I'm giving up gluten."

"Excuse us for a minute," I said, and I blinked for Katie to follow me. We found a quiet spot by the side of the flat-screen TV.

"Who the hell is that in your future?" I whispered.

"I'm really sorry," she said, looking at me. "I do love you."

"But I'm not the guy you want to spend your life with?"

"Ten . . . nine . . . eight," the partiers around us counted as they streamed the feed from Times Square.

"That's not true," Katie said. "You're almost everything I want."

There was no conscious choice about what happened next, just an instinctive recoiling of our bodies, the goose bumps rising against my skin as our layers closed to each other. I couldn't access the lake house anymore or the photos of her father; her childhood dog was gone, followed by the first boy-friend and her college years, until all that was left were my own private memories, trapped deep within my layers, and the pale tint of her skin in the television's light. We were strangers again, and we stood there, looking at each other, while all around us the party counted down the last seconds of the old year.

❋

I LOGGED OFF for long periods after we broke up. I gave up on trying to convince my students to have real-life experiences. When they complained that reading the "I Have a Dream" speech was too boring, I let them stream a thrash-hop version instead, and I sat looking out the window, thinking about Katie. I walked to my station alone every day and sat on the train with my sketch pad, drawing the details I remembered from our trip to Maine: the shoreline with its broken shells and sunlight, the heron before it took flight, Katie's face in the summer darkness. It's the intangible details that I remember the clearest, the ones that there's no way to draw. The taste of the perch as we sat around the table; how a cricket had slipped through the screened windows and jumped around our bed that night; how, after we'd gotten it out, the coolness of the lake made us draw the blankets around us; and how Katie, her father, and I had sat together in the warm light of the living room and played a game, the lettered dice clattering as her father shook the plastic container.

"All right, Andy, you ready?" he'd asked me, holding his hand over the lid.

And I'd thought I was.

ICE AGE

THE IGLOO IS cold this morning. It's been getting chillier ever since we had to cut back on wood rations. But this morning, with the winter winds whistling past our entrance from the north, even the furs don't keep us warm. The kids are already up, playing with snowballs and the Playmobil firefighter I found out on the tundra. I was hunting elk with Tom when I spotted the little red figure. One of the Paulson kids must have dropped it. I bent down, covered it with my glove, and pocketed it. Tom didn't say anything, just kept his eye on the horizon for elk. The way I figure it: the Paulson kids have plenty. My kids, what have they got? Snowballs and a little fox I whittled out of an oak stub.

"Morning," Lisa says. She's cutting up the chinook we've had brining for the past month.

"Morning," I say.

"Hi, Daddy!" the kids say.

And for a moment it all feels good, the four of us in our

igloo with our moose fat candles burning, the morning sun catching the thinner parts of the walls and making a pattern of translucent gray patches in the ice. Lisa brings me a stone bowl of fish and puts another one on the floor for the kids. We sit down on our stones and eat.

"Cold night," she says.

"Yeah. Pray I bag something today."

"Yup," she says, and puts a piece of salmon into her mouth.

Back in the early years we used to talk more. There were emotions to process, loved ones to commiserate over, but eventually, it gets old. You go through all your memories, you tell the same stories, you laugh halfheartedly at stale jokes, and then it's back to silence. The snow has a way of absorbing voices.

When we're done, Lisa gathers the bowls and sits down to sew on the slab of granite we call our couch. She's latching badger fur with fishing twine onto my Carhartts. The kids' playtime is over. They stop their game of covering the Playmobil guy with snow, and Lisa sets them to fixing fishing nets. I get on my hat and gloves and collect my bow and arrows.

"Good luck," Lisa says.

"Good luck, Daddy," the kids say. Then I scoot out of our home.

It's another gray day in our community. The sun's just a dull thump behind the clouds, our scattered igloos like braille against the tundra. The sky spits down flakes, and the wind whirls the frozen drifts into cyclones. The Sanders kids are out in the snow, dragging wood and scraping ice from the branches. We've scavanged most of the usable wood already. The only stuff left is the remaining tops of tall trees that puncture the ice from below, white and frozen. You can chop away at the ice, get a couple more feet of the tree, but it's exhausting work.

Tom's waiting for me by the side of his igloo, his dogs in a huddle, muzzles to tails. "Morning," he says. "Damn cold last night."

"Yeah."

"Fucking Paulsons," Tom grumbles and rouses the dogs.

I don't say anything to that. Enough people already hate the Paulsons that chiming in feels petty. When we first settled the area, the Paulsons kept their distance. They had two Mexicans build their igloo for them: a huge two-story affair, large enough for three families. We built our own shelters, struggling and freezing, as Phil Paulson stacked snowmen with his kids on the horizon. Then the fires started up. Phil Paulson has kept a fire burning *outside* day and night for the past year. You can see the smoke on the horizon, a thin trickle rising into the gray sky behind the high rise of their double-decker igloo.

Tom and some other guys, myself included, went over there early on to talk some sense into Phil about his bonfire. He was out front with his kids, where the workers had built them a snow hill. "Hey there!" he shouted, and let out a whoop as he and his daughters slid down the mound. Round the back of his house you could see the smoke rising from a hole. We went over and looked. The hole was a good twelve feet deep, deep enough to see the splintered wood of a telephone pole, exposed and scorched black by the flames.

Phil came over to our side. "Some weather we're having!" It was an old joke; none of us laughed.

"Phil," I said, "we have to talk to you about this fire."

"Isn't it amazing?" Phil put his hands in his trouser pockets. "I'm figuring in a couple months we'll make it down to the houses. Lots of buried treasure down there."

"You're burning up all the fucking wood is what you're doing," Tom said.

"Please"—Phil looked over his shoulder—"my daughters."

"To hell with your daughters," Tom said. "You're putting out this fire today, got it?"

"Be reasonable," I said, trying a more compromising tone, "you're wasting fuel."

"Guys," Phil said, "I appreciate you coming to talk. Have a safe walk back."

Then Tom tried to take a swing at Phil, and we had to subdue him and lead him back to the dogs.

That night the fire was still burning, so Tom and some other guys went up there, peed on the side of Phil's igloo, and dumped a whole lot of snow down the hole. You could hear the hiss of the coals clear to our igloo. After that incident, Phil's workers installed an insurmountable wall of ice, and from behind the wall the fires started up again. Smelling that smoke, sometimes it's enough to drive anyone crazy.

Tom and I load up the dogs with bear traps, game bait, and our weapons, and let the alpha catch the scent. Today's our day to track. Louis, Doug, and Seth are on wood duty, and Jerry and Sam are on fish. I scan the ice for game. We used to have herds of moose pass by our camp, even the occasional black bear, but animals grow smart when you kill enough of them. In the distance, out by the boulders, I can see a couple black dots, but they could easily be my imagination. The dogs trudge through the snow. It's slow going. The dogs are hungry and tired; most of them aren't even sled dogs, just survivors we trained. Tom and I end up having to get off the sled to walk beside them across the ice, and we make our way toward the boulders, where the rocks rise in sharp cliffs. We set a couple traps, then get downwind and hunch with the dogs behind the rocks.

If it weren't for the ice age, Tom and I would never be friends—if that's what you call two men squatting in the snow clutching bows in silence. Tom and I have fundamentally different souls. I was a cabinetmaker back in the old world. Used to hammer nails, listen to Grateful Dead on a paint-splattered boom box, smoke a joint after work with whichever guys were onsite, and talk about windsurfing as the sun went down. Tom ran an auto supply store where he'd managed to churn himself bitter amid the boxed-up engine parts and jugs of antifreeze. Occasionally, when we're crouching in the ice like this for hours, he'll stare out at the white snow and his face will go slack and he'll say, "God, I could use some blow," letting his memories hang in the frozen air.

Tom lost a lot. The ice storms froze his wife and two children below. Still, we all lost people. Fathers, mothers, friends, life partners. I had a sister out in Reno and a mom and stepdad down in Boca Raton. God only knows where they are now. Frozen far below. Even if they're still alive, I'll never see them again. Boca and Reno are a lot of frozen miles from wherever the hell in Michigan our igloos squat.

We sit and watch the terrain. Nothing moves. The wind whips through the boulders and the sun slides behind the clouds. Snow flurries start and stop, start and stop. Shadows begin to stretch from the rocks. Somewhere far above, a crow caws. And finally the dogs move. They lift their muzzles, huffing at the wind, their ears bristled into peaks.

Tom and I rise slowly. He motions for me to head right as he makes his way down the rock face to another opening. Sure enough, as I look through the gap, there are two moose: a mother and calf nibbling the bark off an exposed treetop. The calf's on my side. I look back to Tom as we notch our arrows. Our eyes meet, we nod, and we fire simultaneously. The calf, hearing the bowstring, looks up and spots me. His legs bend to bolt, but the arrow sinks into him and loosens his body. He attempts to sprint away but his haunches are already weak and he hops clumsily over the rocks, his hoofs clopping against the topsides. The mother follows, and I hear another arrow from Tom's side. The moose snorts, a deep sound of death, and then is gone after her child.

We find the calf far out on the tundra and the mother a bit farther on. The mother's a good-size cow. We split open their bellies and slide the entrails out onto the snow. Tom separates the liver and kidneys, slices out the heart, and puts them in a sack. Then we truss up the cow and calf and load them onto the sled. We check the traps, both empty, before starting back toward home.

With two moose bagged, Tom gets in a talkative mood. "I'll tell you something," he says as we hike across the snow, "Paulson's about to get what's been coming to him."

"Yeah?"

"Me and some other guys are heading up there tomorrow night to put out those fires."

"Good luck. No way Phil's going to let you through the gates."

"He's not letting us; we're axing our way in. I'll put an arrow through him and his wife if they try to stop us."

"Tom, just relax."

"Relax? Freezing's what I'm doing. How about you? You ever spend the night thinking about all the wood the Paulsons have wasted? Your little girls shivering yet?"

"We can move, right? Relocate. Let them have what's left of the woods."

"And leave a perfectly good home to go find another one?

That's plain stupid." Tom spits into the snow. "We've been miles out; there's nothing but ice and rocks."

"The wood will run out anyway."

"Fuck that. Those trees would've lasted us another two years if the Paulsons had let off. Nah, we're going up there and putting an end to this tomorrow night." Tom lowers his head against the winds that howl between us.

"Who's going?" I ask.

"Why? You want in?"

"No."

"Then it's none of your business."

"Don't do it, Tom. They're survivors, like us."

"They're not like us. They don't give a damn about anyone but themselves. Look, you want to extend the olive branch, you go ahead. You're good at talking to people. You go up there and talk to Phil. You get him to put out that fire peacefully, and I'm happy to spend tomorrow night home. But if that fire's burning after sundown, we're going."

We don't speak another word for the rest of the way home. The sun falls low, sending a pink stain across the clouds, and the dogs huff white clouds into the air ahead of us. The other families are happy for our arrival. It's been a good day. A cord of wood has been cut, three trout and a river otter caught, add in our two moose and we've got a feast. The women take the meat into the igloos to prepare it, and we gather together to eat. It's a beautiful night: the smell of singed meat in the air, the children happy as they eat, the snow drifting lightly around us. The scene puts everyone in a festive spirit—enough so that Jerry says he's opening the Disco later that evening and we all should come over.

The Disco was Jerry's baby. He built the igloo and put in a bar with the few bottles of liquor we had among us. Every now and then he'll get some moose tallow candles burning, water down the bottles, and invite us to come dance. Back in the day he had an iPod with a solar charger and he'd play some tunes at the highest volume that little thing could manage. Then the frost bit into Jerry's iPod and shattered the screen. After that it was just the watered-down drinks—so watered down that all you'd really be drinking was colorful melted snow—and the moose candles. You go, drink a couple drinks, and without fail, someone makes a dumbass of themselves by imagining they're drunk.

Still, it was at Jerry's Disco that Lisa and I became a couple. Lisa was one of two remaining single women in the community, the only other one being Martha, a sixty-seven-year-old battle-axe whom we affectionately call Grandma. Lisa's good-looking: large-framed with strong arms capable of skinning moose and hauling ice, tall with big, round mountain-climbing legs and a laugh that rolls from her like thunder. One night I asked Lisa to dance, and it's been her and me ever since. So, I feel like I owe it to Jerry to go to his Disco nights when he throws them.

Lisa, the kids, and I stop in long enough to share a pale yellow cocktail and say goodnight. Then we crawl out and head through the dark cold, the sounds of the community party fading behind us. After the kids are tucked in and dreaming, I tell Lisa about Tom's threat.

"Don't worry, you'll be able to talk to Phil," Lisa says. "You're a good talker."

I don't know why everyone tells me this. All I can remember saying to anyone in the last year is "delicious fish."

So, I try to distract myself like I do when I have insomnia. I think about shopping. For a while, I used to think about food. American breakfasts were my thing: yellow scrambled eggs, thin strips of bacon, sizzling sausages, the mottled golden brown of French toast. But that kind of thinking makes a person wicked hungry, so I switched to shopping. I picture myself pushing a cart down the aisles past Kitchenware, full of waffle irons, pots and pans, spice holders, electric juicers; into Bed and Bath with its hand towels, bath mats, bamboo soap dishes, shower curtains, toothbrush holders; Household and its ironing boards, vacuum cleaners, starch bottles, laundry detergent, peaches, twilight, smoke, moose . . .

I wake to another cold dawn. The kids are outside rolling snowballs down the sloping sides of our igloos. Lisa and I try to give them half an hour of playtime every day so they can experience what childhood feels like. It hurts to think how little time our children get to be kids. Their day is filled with sawing wood, skinning moose, learning to hunt: the work of survival. Lisa gives me the pants she mended and they look good, two strips of badger fur running down the legs. Warm.

I throw some thin strips of marten on the coals, let them sizzle till the gristle starts spitting, flip them over, and drop them into our bowls. We eat, listening to the sound of snowflakes falling outside.

"Okay, I'm going."

"Good luck," Lisa says, and we kiss, our noses brushing against each other's.

Soon I'm out the door, alone, into the long expanse between our community and the Paulsons'. On the horizon their igloo rises, an enormous mound of white interrupting the flat landscape. The snow starts falling heavier, and I hike through the drifts until the ice wall of the Paulsons' towers above me. Through the wall I see the dark shadow of one of the laborers dragging something. I walk around the side where a crude gate has been hewn from a slab of rock.

"*¡Hola!*" I yell over the gate. The figure on the other side freezes. "*¡Amigo! ¡Hola!*" The man puts down what he's carrying and approaches the fence. "*Soy Gordon,*" I yell, trying to recall the little Spanish I still remember.

"Yeah, I remember you," the worker says.

"Oh . . . I'm here to see Phil."

"Why?"

The line had come to me in the middle of the night, a memory from how we used to interact so long ago. "Wanted to invite him for cocktails."

"Wait here," the worker says. I watch him as he makes his way up the stone walkway and through the tall arched entrance of the igloo. He doesn't even have to duck to enter. I wait, kicking the snow and smelling the smoke from the fire as it spools toward the clouds.

Phil emerges from the entrance and heads toward the gate. The chain is unlocked and the large stone slab is opened, and there Phil is, in his woolen vest and trousers, all smiles, his teeth miraculously white and still there.

"Gordon," he says, extending his hand. "Good to see you again!"

"Yeah," I say, shaking his palm with my glove.

"How are the kids?"

"They're fine," I say, taken aback. "I'm surprised you remember them."

"Are you kidding me? Who's going to forget kids that good-looking! So, what brings you up here today?"

"I just wanted to know if you and your wife wanted to come over for drinks this afternoon and talk."

"Well, that's nice of you. Really, we appreciate it. But, to be a hundred-percent honest, Gordy, we don't really like to go down there anymore; hasn't been the warmest reception among the locals. But, hey, we've got plenty to drink here, why don't you come in for a bit? What do you say?"

"Thanks, that sounds good."

Phil steps aside to let me in, and his worker chains the gate behind us. As we walk up the flagstones, Phil's igloo rises above us, thirty-feet high, storm windows set into the snow walls. Through one of the windows I see the Paulson daughters watching me. They raise their hands and wave.

"Sure is nice what you did here," I say.

"Wait till you see the inside," Phil says.

It's true; the interior of the igloo is a work of beauty. Bricks of ice are stacked to form walls, which divide the lower level of the house into a main living room, a kitchen with an attached dining room, a den/office space, and a small bathroom equipped with an oak door for privacy. Along the walls are a series of windows, and around each window a ledge of ice protrudes to create a sill, on which rest framed photos of Phil and his wife playing at the beach. Ice has been intricately cut to form crown moldings and latticework baseboards, and the floor has been covered with white plush carpeting. There's a meticulously chiseled ice staircase leading to the second floor, complete with an ice banister and carpeted steps. What's most striking, however, is the furniture. The living room has a black leather couch and a glass coffee table, upon which the girls are playing with a complete Playmobil fire station: fire engines, the station house, a fire pole, even a little Dalmatian. My kids would kill for that.

"Barb!" Phil calls. "We have company." Barbara appears from the kitchen, warm in mink fur and leggings. "This is our neighbor, Gordon," Phil says.

It's the first time I've met Phil's wife. She's pretty in an old-fashioned way: skinny with too-thin arms that look like they couldn't shovel more than a couple yards of deep snow. Her eyes are black, and for a moment I think it's from sleep until I remember what makeup looks like.

"How nice of you to stop by," she says.

"What are you having?" Phil motions toward the bar. The bottles of the old world are lined up like bowling pins: the squat square flasks of bourbon, dark brown bottles of coffee liqueur, the frosted glass of a vodka bottle. I'm speechless, and it's only when Phil asks again that I tell him bourbon. He fills a tumbler, dropping two ice cubes from a small box beneath the bar, and hands me the drink. I haven't tasted the smoky sweetness of pure bourbon in years, and the flavor shocks my tongue, warming me immediately and answering the question of just how shitty Jerry's Disco drinks truly are.

"How'd you get all this?" I ask.

"That's a good question," Phil says. "And don't worry, I'll let you in on the secret in a minute, but first sit, tell me how life's going down there in town."

So, we sit and talk the kind of talk I'm not used to. Old-world talk about sports and travel. I remember words I haven't heard for ages: public schooling, frequent flyer miles, coq au vin. My blood's so thin from a diet of moose and melted snow that the alcohol hits me hard and I'm dizzy with bourbon and gabbing about dovetailing benches over an empty tumbler when Phil interrupts me.

"Come with me," he says, getting up. "I've got to show you something."

I rise onto tingling legs, feeling a fuzzy kind of love, and follow him back outside and around the igloo to the fire. The cold winds and the smell of smoke sober me enough to remember why I'm here. I have a sudden image of Tom wielding an axe. I promise myself to broach the subject soon.

The hole is enormous, at least twenty feet in diameter and so deep, it's near impossible to see the bottom. From down below, the smoke is steadily rising. There are steps leading down along the outer edge, each step carved out of the snow, a wheel well cut through their center. One of Phil's workers arrives with a wheelbarrow and begins down the spiraling path that corkscrews along the perimeter of the hole.

"Wow," I say. "What's down there?"

"Houses. Only melted our way to one so far, but there are hundreds more. Full of everything you could want. Just last week we brought up a whole set of racquetball clubs. Jorge here says he thinks he can build a relatively decent racquetball court; isn't that what you told me?"

"Yes, Mr. Paulson," Jorge says. He's a shorter man with dark Mayan features and a fuzzy patch of white hair.

"But I'll tell you what made me think of you. There's a garage full of tools down there. Saws, sanders, the whole lot. They're yours if you want them. Come back tomorrow and I'll have Jorge bring them up for you."

"No kidding," I say. "Shame I can't run them."

"Hey, we've got a generator full of gas. Next generator we find has your name on it."

"Wow," I say. Not that there's really anything I could do with the tools. Cut ice into shapes, but still. "That's really kind of you."

"Of course, no problem. How about one moose for it?"

"Huh?"

"I'll give you the tools," Phil says, still smiling, "you give me a moose." His grin is forced now, and I realize his teeth aren't in as good shape as I first thought. His gum line has receded from malnutrition and his cheeks are sunken. It occurs to me that his wife may not have been thin for fashion's sake.

"Phil," I say, "we've got to talk."

"If a whole moose is too much, I'll take parts over time. Think about it. We're talking electricity."

"Gas runs out, Phil."

"There's more gas down there. Plenty of frozen cars. Jorge siphons them out."

"Phil, it's just not how things work around here anymore. You want moose, you have to hunt. Or take part somehow. Your wife, send her down to patch up clothing with the women, or skin badgers."

Phil looks at me in a sorry sort of way. "Gordy," he says, "you don't get to where I've gotten by doing things the way everybody else does them. I'm a thinker, not a hunter. Ideas are what put me ahead."

"Yeah, well, ideas don't put you ahead anymore."

"Sure, they do. You're just not looking far enough ahead.

We can have everything we lost. Maybe not lawns, not yet, but electricity, television, propane; one day I'll open a heated swimming pool, just you wait and see."

"Phil, you're not going to open anything if you don't put that fire out. Tom's insane. He'll be up here tonight if you don't stop the burning."

"Tom?" Phil says, and smiles. "Tom's middle management. The kind of guy you can buy off with a couple bottles of cheap scotch. Trust me, I'm not worried about Tom. I'm talking about you, Gordy. You've got a good head on your shoulders; you want to move up in the world, you'd do good to start thinking for yourself. You get me a moose and I'll get you the first generator I find. It'll put you ahead of everyone. You put in a couple hours hauling up here and I'll let your kids have the first pick of toys in the next house we melt our way into."

I admit it's tempting, the thought of a space heater, a radio, even just a board game to play with my kids at night.

"Look," I say. "This fire can't keep going, you're burning up all the wood."

"Not anymore. Ninety percent of our fuel is coming from the house itself—tables, floorboards, doors—we haven't cut new wood in months."

At first I think he's lying, but I have to admit I can't recall seeing any of the Mexicans out there in the forest since a year ago. Really it's only been rumors of moonlit thefts that have made me think the Paulsons were to blame.

"Put the fire out, at least for a while," I say.

Phil places his hands in his pockets. "No can do. Every-thing will ice up; it'll take weeks to get back to where we were." His other worker is climbing back up with a wheel-barrow full of stuff: tennis shoes, flowerpots, two vacuum cleaners, a chrome electric mixer.

"Don't you get it? They're threatening to come up here to do something really bad. Trust me on this. Just stop the fires for tonight, at least; let Tom see the smoke stop."

Phil laughs. "Tom's sent us plenty of threats before; I'm not worried about him. Listen, you think about what I said. You're a smart man and you seem motivated. That's why I'm offering you an edge. I have to get back to the kids now, but here, take something for the road. Show it to the people down there, let them know what I've got. I'm willing to trade," he says and hands me the KitchenAid mixer. "Jorge, will you show Gordy out?"

"Yes, Mr. Paulson."

"Phil, listen to me. Tom's going to kill you."

"Okay!" Phil says, waving. "Remember, half a moose and I can get you a jigsaw."

Then Jorge's guiding me back around the house and toward the gate. The snow is coming down hard, already covering the stones of the walkway. I brace the KitchenAid against my hip as we walk, wondering what I'm going to do with the thing. Jorge's pace is slower than mine, pinched with the onset of arthritis.

"Were you with the Paulsons during the storms?" I ask Jorge.

"Yes," Jorge says proudly. "Fifteen years I work for Mr. Paulson. You know he saved me before his neighbor. For me he's like family."

"What about your other family? Your real family. Where were . . . *are* they?"

"Chile," he says. "But who knows."

We're at the gate.

"Jorge, what would you do if Mr. and Mrs. Paulson died?"

"That's a sad question, Mr. Gordy. These people, they're like my family now. I guess I'd go try to find my brother."

"Your brother?"

"Yeah, he lives in Iowa."

I don't have the heart to tell him how flat Iowa is, a barren stretch of cornfields with no trees that would have made it above the frost line. There are places where his brother might have had a fighting chance. California, with its great redwoods, the Colorado Rockies, even New York or Chicago, with their monumental skyscrapers, where I imagine survivors camped on the upper floors, scavenging supplies on frigid stairwells. But Iowa? There's no way anyone's still alive out there.

"Iowa's a long way from here," I tell him.

"I know. But still, that's where I'd go. You be careful out there, okay?" he says, and opens the gate for me. "You bring us back some moose, I get you something better than that."

He points at my mixer, whose cord is dragging in the snow. Then he closes the stone gate behind me.

The blizzards have started up again, clouds thick and heavy, the sun blotted out. The snow is falling steadily, whiting out the landscape so I can hardly see a couple feet in front of me. I heft the KitchenAid under my arm, and lumber through the snow crookedly, trudging across the drifts. It's slow going with the wind and snow, the sun so far gone, it could just as well be evening, and I'm chilled by the time I see the dim outlines of our igloos.

Tom's been watching for me. When I arrive he makes his way through the storm.

"Hey," I say.

Tom doesn't say anything, just looks at the KitchenAid and shakes his head. He turns and walks back toward his igloo.

"Tom, wait!"

He pauses. "What?" he says, his back still to me.

There's not enough ice in my heart to do what I should. Not say a word of what Phil proposed, just head back to the quiet of my igloo and keep the kids inside as the men pass through the storm to the Paulsons. If I do that, Tom is liable to kill the Paulsons and loot their home, and by tonight it'll be open season on those houses below. But in that scenario, the Paulsons will be dead, their two daughters orphaned, Jorge abandoned to certain death, and my children get a father who's an accomplice to murder. So, what do I do? I tell

Tom about the houses and all the loot inside. I show him the Kitchen Aid and explain Phil's trade offer, hoping negotiation will quell his bloodthirst. And what more do I do? I call up the old monkey still clinging to his back. "I bet you there's some good painkillers in those houses," I say. I see a momentary flicker, can almost hear the devil on his shoulder whispering beneath the whipping snow; then the light goes out of his eyes.

"Let him talk for himself," he says and spits.

Sure enough, later that night the men organize around Tom's igloo. Am I stopping them? No. But out here you have to choose your battles. If I stand up for the Paulsons, I might as well go build an igloo outside their gate. Still, I can't help but feel horrible as the men crunch by our igloo, dogs barking with the excitement of the hunt, pulling a sled of axes, arrows, and other tools for breaking and bludgeoning.

Lisa and I tuck the kids into bed. I sit and sing our kids to sleep and then Lisa and I huddle together, listening to the snow, both of us complicit in what's going on up there. Even the kids knew. Our eldest had asked me, "What's happening tonight?" "Nothing," I'd lied, smoothing down her hair.

Lisa goes to sleep, but I can't. I sit whittling small figures out of wood for the kids. What I tell myself is, you can only do so much. I did the best I could. I made the hike out there, I told Paulson what was coming, I laid all the facts on the table. It's not my fault what's happening tonight; Paulson made his own decision. You can only do so much, I say out loud. But the words are too quiet, they get absorbed by the snow of our igloo, revealing their emptiness. "Damn it," I say aloud. The last thing I want to see tonight is dead bodies. All the same, I put the little stub of wood down, fold my blade and tuck it away, and put on my jacket.

The sled tracks are easy to follow. I hike through the snow, wondering just what exactly I'm planning to do. Give a speech that warms everyone's hearts? Step in front of the Paulsons with my whittling knife? Still, I continue on, following the deep trench of the sleds through the night, heading toward the dark igloo on the horizon.

The stone door of the entrance is smashed. A quarter of the old slab still hangs from the wall of ice; the rest is scattered across the ground, shards trampled into the snow. There's an eerie stillness to the scene. In the darkness, the unlit sockets of the windows, ominous against the white dome, transform the igloo into an enormous skull. I'm standing there, wondering what to do, when I see someone emerge from the hole. A beam of light cuts through the falling snow, playing over my face and blinding me, and for a second I can't figure out what's happening. It's been so long since any of us had flashlights.

I raise my hand. "It's me, Gordy."

"Hey," Jorge says.

I step through the snow, my boots squeaking against the ice. "Are you okay?"

"Yes," Jorge says and shines his flashlight on the entrance. "But I'll have to build another door."

"Are the Paulsons okay?"

"It was bad for a while, but it's safe now. Everyone's asleep inside. Mr. Paulson's down there." Jorge turns and points his flashlight to the pit. "Come, I'll take you."

Jorge lights the way into the hole and we descend together in silence, circling around the smoke, which rises through the center like a chimney. I stay close to the wall, running my hand along the ice for guidance. Here and there, the cut edges of branches and the scorched wood of a telephone pole emerge from the snow, their feel comforting to the touch. The path flattens out at the bottom and enters a long tunnel of ice. Down here, the ground is brown with mud, speckled with rotten yellow tufts.

"Is that grass?" I ask.

Jorge trains his light on a patch of crabgrass. "Yes, Mr. Gordy. Look here." He lifts the flashlight to the wall by my side. At first I can't see anything, only the glow of his light against the blue ice. But then it all begins to come into focus: the dim outline of a tree frozen within the glacier, a hedge, a long stretch of concrete sidewalk, and the outlines of other houses, dark hulking giants frozen deep within the ice.

"I show you something else," Jorge says. He steps forward a couple feet and disappears into the wall. I follow him down a hollowed-out pathway. We pass the frozen hedge and cross the sidewalk to the side of a parked car. The driver's door is wide open and Jorge shines his light across the interior, illuminating the dashboard, the car stereo, and the sliced balloon of an airbag hanging limp over the steering wheel. The passenger door is also open, creating a kind of vehicular tunnel. It's then that I see what Jorge is really trying to show me: the ice caves on the other side, large open caverns punctured by frozen stalagmites, mailboxes, and the vinyl siding of houses.

"Wow," I say.

"Yes. Come, I'll take you to the others now."

I follow Jorge back to the main tunnel. Ahead of us, the mud turns to flagstones, welcoming us to the gaping door of a ranch house. A small pyre is burning beneath the windows on the left side of the house, melting the way toward a neighbor's. There are voices now, their tone high-pitched but warm, and when we enter the foyer, I see the men from the village inside.

The living room is a memory from the past, long ago forgotten but instantly familiar. The bookcases along the wall, the framed artwork, the carpeting upon which a couch and chairs are arranged, the whole scene lit by candles and upended flashlights, as though set for an intimate dinner party. The dogs are lying on the floor, their muzzles against the carpeting, a couple stretched out on the couch. The men are milling about, stuffing black garbage bags with books and picture frames. They've dragged the sled inside and have stocked it with a floor lamp, a boom box, Christmas lights, and throw pillows. They look like manic shoppers, hoarding the spoils of the old world. Occupied with their pillaging, the men don't notice me, but Paulson does.

"Gordon!" he says warmly. "Good to see you!" He's sitting in a recliner by the fireplace. Tom's beside him in his own recliner, holding a tumbler of liquor in his gloved hands.

Only now do the other men turn. Jerry sees me and waves, sloshing a dark bottle of Myers's into the air. "Disco night!" he yells. The others wave to me before turning back to their work. From down the hallway, I hear the clink of plates in the kitchen.

"You weren't lying," Tom says. "They've got everything down here." He raises his glass in salute to Paulson before downing it.

"Tom's agreed to be my new distributor," Phil says jovially.

"Go ahead," Tom motions to the living room, "take whatever you want. Just make sure to clear it with me before it goes." At this, Tom lifts a clipboard from the coffee table between the two of them.

I don't say anything, just stand there, taking it all in: the smell of alcohol, the men emptying the shelves of knickknacks, the windows white with snow. It's obvious what's about to happen—so clear that, even before Phil offers me a drink, I know what I'm going to do. I'm going to ask Phil where the kids' toys are, and when he tells me, I'm going to get to them before anyone else does. Then I'll take a look at the saws and sanders in the garage. And there will be no blood tonight, no bodies, and no murder among us—just this sled full of pawned goods, and drunken men, spoiling what was once our community.

ACKNOWLEDGMENTS

I am deeply grateful for the love and support of many people. To my parents, for a lifetime of love and guidance. To my son, Peter, the light of my life. Thank you to my agent, Leigh Feldman, and Ilana Masad, for unwavering dedication. My deep gratitude to my editor, the late PJ Horoszko, whose dedication and memory is on every page. Thank you to my publisher at Picador, Stephen Morrison, for believing in my work. To James Meader, Picador's head of publicity, and Isabella Alimonti. Thank you to Tony and Caroline Grant and the Sustainable Arts Foundation for your support of this collection. To Tony Ardizzone, Samrat Upadhyay, and Ross Gay for many years of guidance and friendship. To Bobbie Louise Hawkins, Jack Collom, Junior Burke, and Barbara Dilley for the Naropa years. Special thanks to Phong Nguyen and Michael Kardos, for invaluable guidance on this collection. To Maria, Aaron, and Judy Christoff for supporting me in so many ways. To Jessica Spilos, for all your love and care. To

Robert James Russell, Keith Leonard, Marcus Wicker, Christopher Citro, Abdel Shakur, and Bradley Bazzle for your friendship and edits over the years. To my Danish and English family, for your love and constant encouragement. To Jette & Stephen, Bente & Emilios, and Nicholas (we'll always take the long boat home). Thanks to all my friends who've read my stories, listened to early drafts, and supported me along the way: Sue & Randy, Laura & Jon, Hosef, Tim, Cara, Clay, Tyler, Aquiles, Sherri, Jeremy & Michele, the A2, Geneseo, and Bloomington crew, and a host of others. Thank you to Don Pablo and the Huichol tribe. *Wopila* to Harold Thompson and the Ypsilanti lodge community. And thank you to all the people who are working to make this world a better place.

ABOUT THE AUTHOR

ALEXANDER WEINSTEIN is the director of the Martha's Vineyard Institute of Creative Writing. He is the recipient of a Sustainable Arts Foundation Award, and his stories have received the Lamar York, Gail Crump, Hamlin Garland, and New Millennium Prizes, have been nominated for Pushcart Prizes, and appear in the anthology *New Stories from the Midwest 2013*. He is an associate professor of Creative Writing at Siena Heights University and leads fiction workshops in the United States and Europe.